Santa In My Father's Shoes
And Other Christmas Stories

Printed in Brentwood, Long Island, N.Y.
ISBN 1-885134-07-X

Newsday books are available at special discounts for bulk purchases
for sales promotions, premiums, fund-raising, or educational use.
For details contact:
Marketing Department
Newsday Inc.
235 Pinelawn Road
Melville, N.Y. 11747-4250

Santa In My Father's Shoes
And Other Christmas Stories

Table of Contents

Illustrations by Bob Newman

Christmas Memories

For

_____

From

_____

_____

_____

Introduction

It's a season of sharing, but not just of gifts. It's a time when families and friends share the warmest of memories — the stories of Christmases past.

And for the last 14 years, that's what we've been doing. Every December since 1982, Newsday has published a Christmas essay, each sharing a memory. They are tales told by some of the most gifted storytellers to have written for this newspaper.

Stories like the one from WWII, when Christmas Day for a GI stationed overseas was any day the package from home turned up at mail call. Even if it was October. Or the years when donning the famous red suit in one family meant certain bad luck for the wearer. Or the plane ride with Margaret Mead, when a quiet conversation became a message to parents about believing in Santa. Or the year Santa himself slipped on the rug and the kids thought they'd killed him. (Then he opened his eyes!)

These are the memories of Christmas. The family trudging home through the woods with the less-than-perfect tree. The beloved grandfather whose love of toys made him a Christmas genius. These graceful essays, illustrated each year by Bob Newman, have become a Newsday tradition — a sort of gift to our readers — and one that we hope to continue for many years to come.

Happy Holidays.

— Raymond A. Jansen,
Publisher

Santa Claus And Margaret Mead

by Adrian Peracchio

L arge, wet snowflakes were falling lightly on the ranks of idling taxi-cabs outside the air shuttle termi-nal at Washington's National Airport. I saw her as she strug-gled out of a cab's backseat, lean-ing on her curious forked stick. Even half-hidden by ragged billows of exhaust vapor, Margaret Mead's tiny figure and fringe of white–haired bangs were unmistakable.

I didn't know it then, and she was without a doubt never aware of it, but before the afternoon flight was over, the small, bright–eyed woman with her unassuming air and daunting intel-lect would give me two Christmas presents.

It was the week before Christmas 1976, and we were both returning to New York from Airlie House, a government retreat in the rolling pastures of Virginia's horse country. Three days of seminars and speeches on the future of higher edu-

Santa Claus And Margaret Mead

cation in America: luminaries from the more rarefied strata of academia, stunning boredom punctuated by small flashes of brilliance, droning swaths of jargon as dreary as the lowering skies that offered a gray promise of snow outside the Georgian brick buildings.

The eyes of the men and women in the small press contingent were glazing after the first round of speeches. I flicked through my notebook by lunchtime and counted the word "paradigm" — it had been used more than a dozen times, by three different speakers. "Interface" was very big that year, too. It was a close runner-up.

It took a succinct and pointed speech by Margaret Mead, the woman who had done for anthropology what Carl Sagan would do for astronomy, to dissipate some of the academic cobwebs.

In blunt language, Mead excoriated the higher-education establishment for failing to instill a love of learning in the young. She reminded academics they must nurture the natural curiosity of children instead of deadening it in musty structures.

After her speech, she talked to reporters she knew from the national newsmagazines and the big national dailies. I hovered at the edges of their conversations somewhat diffidently, a young reporter from a New Jersey daily whose quality outshined its public reputation.

At the airport I debated briefly going over to her, and then I dismissed the thought. But when I saw her struggling with her large suitcase after the cabbie had dumped it on the sidewalk, I rushed to offer my help.

She smiled, her eyes sharp and inquisitive. "I've seen you. You were at the place in Virginia, weren't you?" She paused as she walked. "Correct?" I acknowledged it and introduced myself.

"Good," she said. "I don't think I could stand hearing another fellow academic using the word impact as a verb one more time." Later, as we sat together in the plane, she conceded she had been accused of being more of a journalist than a proper anthropologist because of the popular success of her books. "It was meant as a slight, but I usually took it as a compliment," she recalled. "Experts never communicate enough of their knowledge. They keep it to themselves, inside their little circles. They get very jealous of it. That's wrong, of course, but we all do it."

I felt intimidated by the thought of making conversation with a curator and narrator of the Department of Anthropology of the American Museum of Natural History, a pioneer in her field, the author of books I had read as required assignments in anthropology courses. She looked like a kindly grandmother, but there was a hard edge of incisiveness to her words and a tone of voice that brooked no nonsense.

When I began to phrase tentative questions about her career, she gave me a sharp sideways glance and softened it with a grin. "You are not interviewing me, are you?" I told her I wasn't. "You can read all about my past and my work in any good library, young man. And I don't need to have my ego built up. But I don't know who you are. Tell me all about yourself, where do you live, are you married, do you have children, do you like your work?"

Quickly, she extracted from me details I rarely discussed about my life, my growing up and my work. She even coaxed from me an admission that I was worried about the piece I had to do as soon as I got home. In two days I had to prepare a story about Christmas, and I hadn't the foggiest notion what to write about.

"That's easy," she said. "Write about Santa Claus."

"Santa Claus?"

"Yes, you know, Father Christmas, the jolly fat man with the red suit ... "

"Yes, I know. What about him? What's there to write about him?" I wondered if she was mocking me. But her face told me she wasn't.

"Oh, people wonder all the time if they should tell their kids about Santa Claus; they agonize over whether it's good for kids to

Santa Claus And Margaret Mead

believe in someone who doesn't exist. Well, they should stop worrying about it. It's a good myth, a nice myth. Children need to know there is someone who is just good, who comes to them at a special time and rewards them for being good, someone who is not their parent and who exists only to bring joy to them if they've been good. And there is nothing wrong in their believing that they had better follow the rules and be good, otherwise they won't get what they want."

By that time, I had my notebook out and was taking furious notes. She didn't mind it. "You could turn this into a fancy piece of work and go rummaging through other cultures and you'll find there are striking parallels and precedents to the myth of Santa Claus. You can talk about archetypes and that sort of thing, but you don't really have to do that."

The plane had landed and Christmas carols homogenized by Muzak came on the intercom just as the interior lights flicked on.

"There are reasons for these myths, you know," the anthropologist concluded as I helped her with her luggage again. "They have really nothing to do with Christianity, religion or the commercial travesty we have today. They go much deeper than all that. They go to the core of needs we have as human beings, all human beings."

At the curb, she thanked me for my help and, before waving down a taxi, she said in parting, "Think of the children, and write about Santa Claus."

What happened next was predictable: When I brought Margaret Mead's idea to one of my editors, the story began to take on a life of its own. After a couple of news conferences, I was told to track down other cultural anthropologists, get background on the myths of other cultures, interview Bruno Bettelheim, the psychiatrist who had just written a book dissecting the meaning of children's fairy tales. And so on. When the piece was done, it had taken on the faintly smug tone of popular sociology, and had lost the fragile charm of Mead's simple message.

That Christmas, the day I returned home from the trip to Virginia, my wife gave me a fine watch to replace an old and faltering Timex. Engraved on its back is the date. Sometimes when I happen to glance at the engraving, I think of that shuttle flight, and I remember a tiny, white-haired woman in a dark brown overcoat, holding a forked stick and saying as she turned her head to leave, "Don't forget the children. Write about Santa Claus."

When she died, almost two years later at 76, about a month before Christmas, I thought about her message. She had given me two gifts that Christmas. One was small and immediately useful. It had solved my problem of what to write about.

More enduring was the gift of knowing her, however briefly, and discovering that fame and great eminence can exist alongside simplicity and lack of pretension.

Adrian Peracchio *is a member of Newsday's Editorial Board, specializing in foreign affairs. A native of Italy and a veteran of U.S. Army service in Korea and Germany, his previous work included a tour as Newsday's London bureau chief. He was a member of the Newsday reporting team that won a Pulitzer Prize for local reporting in 1984.*

Christmas 1943

by Leslie Hanscom

There was a time, 40 years ago, when the frenzy of Christmas giving used to rise to an early climax in October. Peace on earth there was not, and in every post office, messages in large print gave warning that, if you wanted your soldier or sailor to know that he was remembered at the season when it is saddest to be forgotten, you had better get something in the mail to him by the middle of the month.

Probably at bottom there was wisdom in this summons to early action. Around the world, there were fronts so turbulent, outposts so distant, ships so long out of touch with land that it made sense to allow for the chances of delay. But chance usually worked the other way. The home folks, aghast at the thought their lad in uniform might indeed feel forgotten, obeyed the warnings as though they were commands from F.D.R. himself. The overseas postal service worked with surprising efficiency and the gifts that were mailed in mid–October usually arrived in two or three weeks.

The day the package from home turned up at mail call was, for the average sailor or GI abroad, Christmas Day, no matter what the actual date. The stickers admonishing, "Do not open until...," had about as much restraining effect as you would accomplish if you filled up your dog's dish and pasted a feeding schedule on the side. Packages were ripped open on the instant, cookies and fruitcake were devoured, bottles of cologne were uncorked for the next shave, the paperback novels by Thorne Smith were quickly read through and handed around. When Christmas Day actually came, the GIs knew they hadn't been forgotten — but they couldn't remember how they had been remembered.

The Yuletide of exactly 40 years ago was, for the party who is now reminiscing, the first one away from home. If I had hung up a stocking that year — as a scant 10 years before, I would routinely have done and still half–believed that it was Santa Claus who would do the rest — it would have been a sock of an olive–drab color. It would have hung by a sleeping bag on a folding canvas cot, and it no doubt would have invited ribald comment from the other inhabitants of a Quonset hut, buried below the wind in the tundra of a dismal island in the North Pacific.

I hung no stocking, but I did entertain another childish impulse. On the day in early November when my Christmas bounty arrived in a battered carton, I took out the gifts and, instead of husking them of the wrappings then and there, I spread them out on the cot and gave in to hesitation. I longed to have them for the day properly appointed. Thinking ahead to a Christmas Day which, as far as I knew, would be barren of anything to make it special, I wanted to hold onto these tokens of home and open them ceremonially at the right time.

The folly of doing this I well knew. The other denizens of the crowded hut were already sniffing the packages for their cut of whatever edible material might be in them, and I foresaw what colorful shortcomings of manhood I would be accused of if I indulged my sentimentality and made them wait.

Then, in the manner of a Christmas miracle, I was rescued. Mine wasn't the only bundle from home to arrive that day. The other had come to the member of our squalid little household who was the senior in years and who was held in automatic respect by all hands for this and better reasons. Ferris was a lanky, agreeably homely young man with red–blond hair, who held a sergeant's rating for manning a gun on the crew of a B–24 bomber. He was probably around 28 years old, which made him half a generation older than I was. I looked up to him as a grownup, which he was and which he showed by extending an instinctive protectiveness toward those who were greener in years and less secure in their bearings

As I sat equivocating over my heap of Christmas gifts, nervously aware of the wolverines who were waiting for me to act, he seemed telepathically to sense what was going on in my feelings. Loud enough for all to hear, he announced from his end of the shack that he had just come to the decision that instead of immediately rifling his own gifts, he was going to do it the right way and save them for Christmas. Happily relieved by this mode of deliverance, I blurted that I was going to do what Ferris was going to do. Since all of us believed that whatever Ferris did was what ought to be done, this was received with a minimum of murmur.

Ferris had achieved his place of dignity among us by his unmistakable maturity. It was his gift for smoothing troubled waters that enabled us to live at such close quarters with an almost unbelievably small amount of friction. He kept the card games good–natured

Christmas 1943

and the arguments on a plane of reasonable debate. In the sympathetic kindness that was a reflex with him, he not only allowed me, as the youngest of the bunch, to participate in conversations, but would draw me in if I hung back, even though in my unfinished condition at the time, I didn't have much to contribute. Once when I was humiliated to have it pointed out to me that I kept a deplorably gummy razor — partly because I didn't have to use it every day — he made light of this by defining dirt to me as nothing more than "misplaced matter." Strange to recall, at home in Cleveland he was a cop.

If there is any reason for bringing this unmomentous Christmas memory to mind, it is mainly to remember him. Except for his unusual sensitivity to the feelings of other people, he seems to me now to typify, in his ordinariness and decency, the generation which fought that war. We who belonged to it had been raised on movies that, instead of celebrating depravity, exalted in their corny way the virtues of self-sacrifice and heroism. We put on the uniforms to make our parents proud of us and of the service star hanging in the window.

There were no questions in our minds about the rightness of it. The theater of action that is the setting of this reminiscence might have raised some questions. Those who were posted there were on an inglorious and Godforsaken fringe of the global combat. Their part of the grand design was to harass the Japanese islands from the north, and for this purpose, a squadron of bombers was stationed on a dot of U.S. territory near enough to the Japanese's to bring the enemy within range of aircraft that now seem primitive. The men who flew the missions had two adversaries to withstand — the Japanese and, far more dangerous, the abominable weather of the region.

At the time of year when Christmas drew near, missions were rare because the daylight in that latitude was short. If the caprices of the weather turned favorable, however, the chance was too precious to miss. It was thanks to an unaccustomed day of calm 40 Decembers ago that the crew to which Ferris belonged was summoned to go aloft on a rickety old "flying boxcar" that bore the name of Polka Dotty.

As usual, he buckled himself into his sheepskins with no nerves showing. One of the reasons he commanded so much respect was that, although he was probably as much in dread as everybody else at the outset of one of these assignments to suicide, he kept it to himself. When a mission was about to go out, a line usually formed at the shack that served a sanitary purpose, because fear has a way of gathering in the intestines. I don't remember ever seeing Ferris in it. He seemed to be in control even of that part of himself.

Even though it was a rare — and all too temporary — glimpse of sun that caused Polka Dotty to be sent out that day, I remember it as a day of darkness growing dimmer to an ultimate pitch of gloom that arrived at a certain point in early evening. This was when the chief of Polka Dotty's ground crew — called "Pap" because, at 22, he had the slow ways of an old man — slouched into the hut, threw his sheepskin jacket against the wall and himself on his cot. He lay on his side with the tears running off his big nose as he delivered the news from the radio operators on the ground that Polka Dotty wouldn't be coming back.

The card game went on as usual in the hut that evening, but there wasn't much talk. Players, kibbitzers and lookers-on gathered at a different cot from the one where the game usually took place. That was the cot that everybody was trying to look away from. It stood in the shadows cast by the gas lantern that was our only light, but all too glaringly visible underneath it was the pile of gifts waiting for Christmas morning.

When that morning eventually came, I did it Ferris' way, opening my gifts at the ritual time by the light of a candle. The sun wouldn't be up until a couple of hours or so before noon, and nobody else was in a hurry to be awake.

I was glad that the others slept because there was no mer-

7

riment in the performance. The other collection of gifts was still there, and I couldn't get rid of the thought that, if it weren't for a gesture which I thought the owner of them had made for my benefit, he might at least have known in what way his parents and his girl-friend had remembered him before he died.

It is strange to recall that, as Christmas came and went, nobody made a move to molest the heap of gifts. For all of the rapacity with which my companions in arms had attacked their own and would have ripped into mine, they didn't invade this little sanctuary. I can't remember how the effects of the deceased were disposed of in those circumstances, but whoever took away Ferris' belongings left the gifts behind, and they stayed in their place as we moved into a new year and longer daylight.

Eventually, somebody new arrived to occupy the cot that had been his, and space had to be cleared for the gear of the newcomer. Those of us who remembered the older occupant gathered up the gifts and put them in another place. At the door of the hut, we had built a storm entry out of wood swiped from the Navy base and grandly equipped it with shelves. The gifts were placed on one of these, and they stayed there as the lashing snowstorms of winter turned into the lashing rainstorms of spring.

If this were fiction, I could bring the story to a satisfying conclusion by reporting that the lost man was mysteriously found and that he came back to claim and enjoy what we had saved for him. Of course, it didn't happen, so the memory has to end in a somewhat feeble way.

With the coming of spring, the grand strategists who ran the war and the destiny of us of lower rank determined that the squadron would perform more usefully if based on another island. Responding to orders, we packed our gear and prepared to leave a ghost town of the place that for a time had been the center of our world. On a day when the ship was waiting at the dock, the hut I remember was stripped so empty that it seemed pointless even to close the doors as we departed.

With a rucksack on my back, I started down the hill to the dock and then some paces on the way, remembered that there was after all a reason to draw shut a door. It was, as usual, raining, with the wind blowing the sheets of water in the horizontal way characteristic of our beloved local climate. Ferris' Christmas presents were exposed to the rain. I went back and closed the door of the storm entry to keep them protected in the place where, for all I know, they may still repose.

Is this a pointlessly sad little reminiscence to bring up at a happy season? Probably so, except that Christmas is an emotional time, and to those of us now graying into senior citizenship, the memories that carry the heaviest freight of emotion have to do with the years I am recalling. For me, it also has a significance that I can cite as an apology.

I am remembering these incidents after 40 years partly because they turn on the pivot of one tiny, offhand, humane gesture. The man who made it has been gone from the Earth longer than he was on it. He is probably more appropriately remembered by people who knew him better, like the givers of the gifts. That I remember him, however, and that he comes back so vividly every year when the signs say, "Mail early," seems to say that kindness is seldom wasted — which isn't a bad thing to bear in mind at Christmastime.

Leslie Hanscom joined Newsday in 1970 after a career that had included jobs at the Brooklyn Eagle, the World Telegram & Sun, Newsweek, The Saturday Evening Post and the Philadelphia Inquirer. A native of Maine, he served in both the U.S. Army and the Peace Corps. He was Newsday's books editor and a books columnist before retiring in 1988.

Bringing Home The Tree

by Fred Bruning

We bought our Christmas tree at the fire department this year because the Episcopal church sold its stock so quickly. If the firehouse boys or some other nice, nonprofit group hadn't been able to offer a decent choice, we would have surrendered to one of the commercial lots, although grimly. I've had a terrific aversion to those quick-buck places since a tree jockey in Queens nearly took a poke at me a few years ago. He objected to my asking another shopper the price she had been quoted — a serious breach of ethics on a lot where nary a

Bringing Home The Tree

price tag was to be seen.

"You don't ask a customer," said the fellow, big, angry and almost upon me. "You ask a salesman."

"I was just trying to find out how much," I answered in a register that made me sound ready for the Vienna Boys Choir. My two sons and the playmate who had come along to help choose a tree were wide-eyed. As if on signal, they began edging toward the exit, and I did too.

Actually, I knew I might cause trouble with my unauthorized pricing survey. Upon walking onto the lot, I aroused suspicions by noting aloud that the trees were not marked. Almost certainly I then delivered one of my timeless lectures on consumer awareness, though I cannot recall the details. Tapping the woman on the shoulder made matters worse. Boldly drawing her into my scheme was, for the proprietors, an act no less provocative than the assassination of Archduke Ferdinand.

"You want to know how we set the price?" said the big fellow, now joined by a colleague who seemed in no better mood. "We charge according to your face. We like your face, it's one price. We don't like your face, it's another price." As if there were any doubt, he added with some finality: "We don't like your face."

The kids and I were at the curb when the salesman warned I would be spending Christmas in St. Somebody's intensive care unit should I come 'round again. How could I tell him how little chance there was of me returning? Sooner I would buy an aluminum spruce at Alexander's or move the clothes tree into the living room and drape it with sashes from our several bathrobes. In the end, we bought a sturdy fir from vendors who had staked out territory beneath the elevated portion of the West Side Drive — a Depression-era scene straight from the set of "Annie." I can't remember if the wares were tagged. By then, who cared? The next year, we began doing business with the Scout troop in our neighborhood and, later, as

suburbanites, the Episcopal church.

I mention all this by way of clearing a path to a happier sort of Christmas tree experience. There is no real connection between the two, except in my mind, except in the way that happy memories are fused by some law of cosmic physics to recollections we might sooner forget.

The fellow in Queens has assumed, in our family, a kind of celebrity status — a sort of real-life "Grinch Who Stole Christmas." As such, he is a useful character. He is our favorite villain, and the very thought of him growling and gesturing and threatening to dismember me summons an equal and opposite force of equanimity. I suppose one might argue that Christmastide is the season for such peculiar reactions, for it is the time when we expect somehow that innocence and wonder will prevail, at least until the ribbons and bows are cleared away and the feasting yields to heavy sleep — until the next day dawns, the pace quickens and the world is what it is, again.

Courtesy of Mr. Grinch, a very tough guy, we go back then — back, back, nine years back. Back to Vermont, to that place of long underwear and maple sugar shacks and whole-wheat doughnuts and hay bales, rutted roads, red fox, glare ice, cow pies, and to a queer-looking white house in a frozen swatch of pasture. Ah, yes, Grinch, old fellow, back we go to 1975 and Groton, Vt.

The house is cold. The house is always cold. Blissfully — and voluntarily — unemployed for a year, we are living in Vermont on a driblet of money and must conserve everything, especially fuel oil. The thermostat can be set no higher than 60. In real degrees, that buys you a 58 — less when the sun goes down.

We are, all six of us, in heavy clothes from morning to eve. Turtlenecks, sweaters, flannel shirts — layers and layers of clothing that make us look like a family of bears. Mama, Papa and the four cubs. When friends come to visit from New York or Massachusetts, they laugh, heh-heh, at the chilliness, as if to say: It's a joke, right?

Bringing Home The Tree

Don't ask us to believe you actually cope with this.

At last, visitors accept the idea but often refuse to take off their coats. "No, no, that's all right," they'll say jerking the arms of their jackets away. "I'll just wear it, if you don't mind." In parkas they sit around the kitchen table over steaming cups of coffee looking more like a polar expedition than city folks come north for fresh air and a few rounds of Scrabble.

As for us, we are used to it — or at least have come to believe we will survive our freezer-chest existence. By the second week in December, the sloping farmland outside our rented place is lacquered with snow. On sunny days, the brilliance has the incendiary quality of a nuclear test. Clear nights, hillsides glow with the luminosity of stars.

Wind tumbles over the sheet-metal sections of our steeply slanted roof and slips inside the plastic window covering. We listen to the local radio station every morning and thrill at the word of early temperature readings: 1 above; 2-, 12-, 18-, 23-below! The children, all in elementary school, gulp their oatmeal or pancakes and pull on jackets with the determination of defensemen affixing helmets before a goal-line stand. Off they trudge, heels squeaking in the snow, heads turned against the wind, marching wordlessly to the spot on the hard-packed county road where Mr. Bickley will stop the school bus.

Later, after breakfast dishes are done, the adults venture out, too. Groceries, the newspaper, the bank. Any excuse. It is essential not to feel held in place by the whistling wind and radio reports, not to contemplate the tundra, tug glumly on the sleeves of your sweater and say: "Whoosh, really blowing out there. Better stay home."

Without jobs, we have nothing to nudge us, unwillingly, into the snow and wind. But we do not want to return to New York next summer and say that mostly we sat around and ate Hershey's kisses or slept late, or worst of all, that we became TV freaks — not much of a danger, to tell the truth, since in this uncabled part of the country, only one channel is received.

Having decided, then, to embrace the environment insofar as reason and our megalopolitan backgrounds would permit, we announce to the kids a few days before Christmas that we will, after lunch, hike into the woods across the road and there pluck a tree from nature's bounty. From our windows, the pine forest looks dense — awesome but inviting. Our choices will be endless.

Something short of jubilation breaks out. For all the fortitude they show on frigid mornings, the children have not exactly developed into fur trappers or native guides. They lack entirely the urge to wander past the apple trees out back or tramp along the fence line at the far end of the pasture. There is a lovely brook in that direction, and we presume upon arrival in late summer that the kids will make a beeline for anything that promises to keep them cool and their sneakers wet. Perhaps because they need time to adjust to the place, or perhaps because they just have better things to do, they never head for the stream, nor for any other point much removed from home. Only our dog, the intrepid George, habitually extends the family parameters. We see him sniffing at the ground in the distance and cantering on the knolls — a suburban creature enjoying the splendors of a world undisturbed by chainlink fence, highway traffic or local dogcatcher.

There is minor debate regarding the wisdom and necessity of the Christmas tree search, but authority prevails, as it so often does, and we suit up. It is brisk outside, and while not the sort of icy cold that stuns the face and causes the throat to ache, the temperature keeps our breath hovering in the air like a fog of hummingbirds. Huffing, puffing, letting off steam, we move out single file looking like an odd sort of locomotive departing some country station. Small wheels in front, the larger in the rear, groaning to make momentum.

We chug across the country road, skirt a small frozen pond and negotiate the strip of pasture where until mid-autumn, the dairy herd belonging to Ken and Barbara Murray had lolled and flicked ears at flies and, on occasion, broken into a thundering gallop as though auditioning for an old-fashioned Hollywood western.

The snow is deep here, deeper than we expected, and progress is slow. Our troops are quiet, resigned to their fate, at least for the moment. "How far are we going?" someone asks.

"Oh, just a little farther," comes the reply.

"Sure. I bet."

We are starting up the rise. It is a gentle incline, which, within a half mile, will give way to a crest and then the pine grove. We pause more often now and look back toward our rented house as a means of gauging distance traveled.

The house is a fine place, really — a white clapboard affair so cleverly designed that the passerby cannot tell easily if it is an old farm building that has been renovated or a new structure indebted to traditional shapes. From this distance though, the house, which, in fact, is only a few years old, looks ordinary enough, a kind of cockeyed snow drift that might have been standing for centuries in some endless, flash-frozen landscape. The day is gray — the color of our sheet-metal roof — and it registers on me that the temperature is dropping. Even the meager warmth in our solitary house across the road would be welcome.

On we go.

When we reach the forest, the kids begin assessing trees — Here's one! What's wrong with this? Whadda'ya looking for, anyway? — but we urge them to walk with us a bit more. Around here somewhere is the gravity-fed contraption that sends water all the way back to the house. We'd had trouble with our supply a couple of times and wanted to inspect the rig just so we'd seem a little less dopey when the subject next came up with the Murrays. Ken and Barbara know everything about land, cattle, maple syrup, automatic milking machines, firewood, school closings, dead batteries and gravity-fed water systems. As the Murrays cheerily insist at every opportunity, New Yorkers know a lot less.

Ahead, the land drops into the shape of a trough. We spot the stream and the cistern. Our exotic gravity-fed "system" is a ridiculously simple device composed of concrete cylinder, strainer and rubber hose. No one is impressed.

By this time, the kids are approaching the point of mutiny. Hurriedly, we get to work, inspecting one tree after another for shape, height, fullness — a discouraging task. What had looked like a forest of heavily boughed beauties from our living room window turns out to be a collection of nature's rejects. The trees are short, scrawny and strangely shaped. Somehow we have wandered into a forest of wimps.

"Where's the good trees?"

"Can't we buy a better one?"

"They're ugly."

"I don't like 'em."

Now the whole circus is gearing up. Our eldest child becomes convinced there is a bear in the woods and enters the first stage of shock. Our No. 2 takes offense at the remark of a sibling, decides she has endured quite enough nonsense for one day, and announces she will hike back without our company. The two youngest want only to bring the ordeal to an end.

"This one," they demand.

"This one?" my wife and I say, weakening.

"Yes."

And so, from beneath my jacket I produce a cross-cut saw, and in no time we fell the tree of 1975. Its toothpick trunk offers little resistance, and when it topples, there is no sound. Does a tree exist if it falls without a thud? Don't ask.

Carrying the tree would not be difficult, but it seems like we ought to drag our trophy through the snow if appearances are to be maintained. Out of the forest we march and into the clearing. Fifty feet ahead, our daughter leads the way, accompanied by George, the dog, who no doubt is getting an earful regarding family dynamics and the perplexing, parental notions of what constitutes fun.

Bringing Home The Tree

Our first-born, the least inclined toward physical exertion and the most attuned to grizzlies snorting in the mythical distance, is hurrying us along now that we are on a downhill track. We are sniffling and hacking. Our faces are red. The sky is soot-colored.

Inside the house, we drink hot chocolate and, later, without much enthusiasm, attend to the tree. I string the lights and attach the star to its spindly top. The kids load on the ornaments. Then come garlands and a little tinsel — a yearly exercise that proceeds without blueprint or very many words.

Outside, the world seems smothered by darkness. There is no moon, and the Earth is dim without it. The treeline across the meadow is a faint stroke on the horizon. Just barely, we can see the top of the hill and the pine forest, but our tracks in the snow are invisible.

"Well," I say, "let's put it on."

I push the plug and the living room feels immediately warmer, as though a tropical breeze suddenly has floated by. The children look at what we have done and silence holds us for a moment. Against the white walls of the house and the great darkness beyond, the lights blaze — red, green, orange, blue. Windowpanes reflect the cheery scene. There we are, the six of us, glistening like candies in the tinted light. Curiously, the image seems to have been projected, like a transparency, through the glass, as though our enormous white meadow were serving as screen for some future family slide show.

"It looks all right!" says someone.

"It does."

"Yeah, looks good."

"It looks … beautiful."

On Christmas both grandmothers visit. We write a play for the occasion, and all take part, even George. The grandmothers say everything is swell — the house, Vermont, the Christmas cookies, the kids in their pajamas, the dog, the fireplace, the tree. The tree? We bring the grannies to the window and point to the crest and the pine forest. That tree? We cut that tree down ourselves.

We tell them how cold we were and how far we walked and how the snow got into our boots. We tell them about the cistern and the bear sounds and how George rambled through the countryside like a husky. We tell them the radio said it had been 4 degrees around the time we took our hike. We shiver for effect. The grandmothers look at us, and, as though in agreement, they shiver, too.

*   *   *

After Vermont, we moved to the city and then, five years later, back to the suburbs. Often enough, though, we head to New York for a visit and often enough, too, we pass the corner fruit stand in Queens, where, during Christmas season, trees are sold from an adjoining lot.

"There it is, Dad," my youngest son remarks so frequently that I know the memory of that day is fresh for him. "Do you remember? Do you remember that guy?"

I tell my son that, yes, I remember the guy. Mr. Grinch. How could I forget?

Surely, the man would be amazed to learn how important I have allowed him to become, how much a part of the season. I wonder, if I encountered him deep in some December, whether it would be foolish or inappropriate to call out a greeting as though to an old friend?

"Merry Christmas," I might say, hoping my voice achieved respectable tone and strength.

He wouldn't recognize me, of course. Why should he? "Merry Christmas," the fellow might answer. "Merry Christmas to you."

Fred Bruning, who first joined Newsday in 1969, has worked for papers in Albany, N.Y., and Miami, and for Newsweek magazine, and currently is a writer on the Newsday features staff. His work also appears in many magazines, and he writes a monthly column, "An American View," for the Canadian newsweekly Maclean's.

The Silent Caroler

by Joe Gergen

I never sang "O Holy Night!" Not in public, that is. If it wasn't quite the disappointment to me that it was to my family, that's because I genuinely felt my talent for music was best served as a listener.

But our household was in possession of a piano, one which my mother and aunt delighted in playing, especially in those years before Milton Berle and his television cohorts moved into the living room. My mother and aunt claimed to play the piano "by ear." My observation, which I dutifully kept to myself, was that my aunt's ears sometimes had difficulty in choosing

The Silent Caroler

from among so many eligible keys.

At a young age, I was summarily entrusted to the care of an aged nun for the purpose of piano lessons. I was to be the first in the family to read music before committing my hands to the ivory. Alas, the choice of reading material was not inspirational.

The focal point of music in our semi-attached Queens house, located directly across the street from a Catholic church, rectory, school and convent, was Christmas. Frequently, my mother and aunt would sing along with the piano, keeping their lungs in shape for the choir that always made midnight mass on Christmas Eve such a special occasion. Naturally, I was expected to follow in their voice tracks.

But back to the piano. The song with which the good sister sought to indoctrinate this antsy neophyte was "Believe Me If All Those Endearing Young Charms," a treacly piece at best, which sounded much worse when dragged bar by bar through the doldrums of the learning process. After a month or two, I began to gag on the tune. After several months of practice on the piano in the living room, my mother and aunt began to gag as well, perhaps because their ears were the very instrument of their musical aptitude.

It didn't much matter that I began to pick up speed, that in time I was playing the wretched melody at something approaching its suggested tempo. The sister wouldn't give me another piece until I had mastered this one. And before that happened, it was the consensus of my mother, my aunt and myself that none of our ears — including mine, which had yet to be educated — could stand any more abuse. Thus did my career at the piano end, considerably short of the classic Christmas material whose sheet music had been stored in the bench in preparation for my development.

Fortunately, for the others, I still had my voice. And a nice voice it was in those days, suitable for the children's choir. With the proper coaching, it was thought, I might someday be able to per-

form the solo that was the high point of Christmas mass every year, "O Holy Night!"

That seemed a preferable alternative to the piano, in any case. But a strange thing happened one day in the course of a stickball game. When called upon to shout, the voice cracked. It did so again and again. And, during the next rehearsal for the choir, the moderator heard several discordant notes emanating from my larynx.

Thus was the advent of puberty acknowledged. I was henceforth consigned to a group known as the Bluebirds, who were invited to open their mouths in song as long as they remained quiet. Silent night, indeed.

Left with no musical options, I dutifully devoted more time to activities as an altar boy, where it was required only that you speak and not sing responses. True, the responses were in Latin, but that was more a function of memory than any real understanding of a foreign tongue. Altar boys also had their place at midnight mass. It was in folding chairs on a side altar directly in front of the sisters whose eyes seemed to burn through the surplices and cassocks that were our uniforms and into our mischievous hearts and conspirational minds.

Our primary duty at the service was to be seen and not heard, certainly the most difficult of assignments for healthy youngsters 11, 12 and 13 years of age. We marched into position to the wordless commands of a nun, who pressed on a clicker in her palm when we were all to genuflect, stand up or sit down. The standing could be hazardous if a friend behind you happened to tuck the folds of your surplice into the hinges of the chair. The clatter was quite audible even beyond the front row occupied by the sisters.

There was one other significant threat to peace on Earth for the altar boys at midnight mass. And that was the music. The choir was excellent. The concelebrants were adequate in voice. But the pastor, an old monsignor, was as hard of singing as he was of hearing.

It must have been a strain for him to attempt the high

The Silent Caroler

notes. Lord knows, it was a strain for some of the listeners to keep a straight face. Invariably, one snicker in our group would start a chain reaction. The difficulty then was trying to stifle it, or at least confine the giggles to the left side of the face which was, we believed, out of sight of the all-observant figures in the first row. Woe be to those suspected of desecrating this most joyous occasion with laughter.

As a result, Christmas music was a rich mixture of pleasure and guilt. And, in later years, it became a reminder of both the animation and constraints of childhood. But, like all things frequently sampled, it gradually lost its impact. The Christmas season, with its demands for shopping, addressing greeting cards and stringing lights, was such a distraction. There seemed so little time for listening, let alone hearing.

And so it was until that Sunday afternoon in the winter of 1984. We were on vacation in Israel, my wife and I, and we were making the last stop on our last tour before flying home. The bus stopped in Manger Square, Bethlehem.

We had, of course, attempted to see too much too quickly. In the span of six days, we had floated in the Dead Sea and sailed on the Galilee, looked down from Masada and stared up at the Golan Heights. Lynn, who is Jewish, saw the Old Testament wherever she looked. Raised a Catholic, I was more familiar with the New.

So we honored her traditions with prayers at the Wailing Wall and mine by following the Friday afternoon procession along the nearby Via Dolorosa. We saw Mount Zion and the Mount of Olives, we journeyed to Hebron to visit the burial ground of the patriarchs Abraham, Isaac and Jacob, and we drove by winding mountain roads to Nazareth, site of the Annunciation and the place where Jesus was raised.

All of it was memorable and all of it was committed to color photographs. But the last stop, following a quiet moment at Rachel's Tomb, was particularly moving for both of us. We followed the guide inside the Church of the Nativity.

The purpose of our visit lay behind the altar, in a crypt. People gathered around a flame set in the marble floor, at the spot where Jesus was born. They held candles in their hands.

Suddenly, a new group entered. They arranged themselves around the sanctuary and, without a word being spoken, began singing "Silent Night." It was mid-March. It was Christmas.

I looked at my wife. Her eyes were filled with tears. I thought of those midnight masses so long ago. Once the pilgrims had finished their song and moved on, my inclination was to sing aloud "O Holy Night!," whose occasional performance in the last three decades had been limited to the shower.

I stifled it. As inspiring as was the setting, it couldn't make a songbird out of a Bluebird.

Joe Gergen was born in Brooklyn and graduated from Boston College, where he was the sports editor of the student newspaper. He has been a sports columnist for Newsday since 1975 and has published four books, including "Kiner's Korner" with Ralph Kiner.

Santa In My Father's Shoes

by Anne Raver

When Linda Grady told me there was no Santa Claus, I just figured she was what Grandmother called "limited."

We were coloring dittoed pictures of Santa in Miss Sprinkle's first–grade class and I'd asked to borrow Linda's black crayon. She was the kind of girl who never lost hers.

She turned around in her seat in front of me and said, "You don't know, do you?" If I'd known the word, I'd have called her smug.

Santa In My Father's Shoes

"What?" I said, staring at her saddle shoes. They were brown and white and I wanted them.

I took her black crayon, which she kept sharpened, and began drawing a pair of glasses on Santa's face. He'd worn them as long as I'd known him.

I could feel her looking at me. Even at 6, Linda had the weighty stare of a Sunday School teacher.

"There isn't any Santa. That's what," she said flatly. And turned around again.

I stared at her pale, plump elbows and felt happy she was getting fat. Then I went back to my coloring.

I knew Santa existed because he came to our house every year. First you'd hear the sleigh bells, far off in the sky. Then his voice, calling to Blitzen. He loved Blitzen more than the others, for some reason, which was the way with families, like Dad loving my eldest brother the most. Then, so loud, it felt like thunder inside your chest, he pounded on our big front door. The youngest — me — had to let him in.

Poor Linda. In that way grownups have of letting you know, without ever putting it into so many words, it had been made clear to the Raver kids that the Gradys were an honest and upstanding sort of people, but totally colorless, almost pitiable in their inability to believe in anything extraordinary. This was why Linda always got gold stars for her coloring projects. She never went outside the blue ditto lines.

Christmas at our house was kind of like some church group deciding to stage a Wagnerian opera. Nobody could reach high C, but our enthusiasm shattered glass. The absolute climax was Santa's arrival on Christmas Eve, but everything that went before was the real story.

It started with Grandmother hauling out her ancient tin cookie cutters and mixing up this molasses glop in a yellow bowl about as big as a washtub. These cookie cutters had been made by Great-Granddaddy, who fought on the Monitor during the Civil War. Actually, he'd just done the woodworking or something, but we liked to say he'd fought on it, and after all, there was a picture of him in Grandmother's room looking very handsome in his Yankee uniform.

"Now where in the Lord's name am I going to put this?" she'd say, opening the refrigerator and squinting at the little bowls of creamed chipped beef and leftover kale and limp salad that were precariously balanced on packages of scrapple and bacon and candied fruit, bottles filled with mustard and old vitamin pills.

"Why look here, Kathleen," she'd say to Mother, who was busy on her side of the kitchen making Aunt Dolly's brownies or Florence Earp's sand tarts. "Weren't you looking for the horseradish yesterday?"

Somehow they'd wedge that dough into the refrigerator, where it would sit overnight and turn into cement. Then, with her powerful arms, Grandmother would roll out the dough, and my sister and I would cut out the cookies.

This would have been a tedious project, had not Grandmother allowed herself to be persuaded to tell about the mean-hearted foster girl who burned down the barn because she was so jealous of Pauline, the other foster girl, who was Grandmother's favorite. Actually, to hear how both orphans had to work on the farm, daily thanking the Lord that Grandmother had saved them from the life of unimaginable sin that she hinted existed in Baltimore, they should have joined forces and thrown their slave driver into the barn before they struck the match. But she was a lot of fun in other ways.

"Tell us about the fire," I said, slipping our dog, Joe, a lump of raw dough.

"Don't give that slobbering animal my good dough," she said. She and Joe glared at each other for a few seconds. We'd rescued this grumpy old boxer from the rather disturbed life he'd been leading on the end of a chain at the local gas station, and he was a good match for Grandmother.

She cinched her apron tighter around her broad hips.

"Oh, you don't want to hear that old story all over again," she sighed.

This was our cue to say something like, "Didn't she come from Montrose?" Montrose was a home for "wayward girls" that made Jane Eyre's school sound like Briarcliff.

"Yes, that's right, I went up there myself to get her, and she was a little bit sullen, you know, but I didn't want a chatterbox either," Grandmother would say.

Then she'd be off. How the girl was smart enough to let all the water run into the barn trough for hours before she set the fire, so that when everybody woke up in the middle of the night and stumbled out on the kitchen porch to stare at the flames already clear up to the sky, and the men ran down to the barn to try to get the animals out, and the horses were screaming and so confused they kept running back into the flames, and Granddaddy shouted to Grandmother, "Grace! Start the pump!" — not a drop came out.

And so on. Such rituals continued for days. Using a hammer, Dad pounded the fresh coconut for the cake and ordered everybody around until there were violent arguments and slammed doors. Nobody could agree on how many kumquats went into the cranberry sauce. We'd smooth the waters with a few carols, Grandmother at the piano, the rest of us honking and squeaking along on instruments we hadn't practiced all year.

We'd ponder whether to look over in Frank Fenbe's woods for the Christmas tree or cross the stream over to Elijah Blizzard's.

"I don't know," Mother said. "Since Joe got into Elijah's chicken coop last summer, he's been a little curt with me." Joe had scared the hens so bad they hadn't laid any eggs for weeks.

Of course, if we went over Frank's way, we risked a discussion about religion. Ever since he'd seen Mother doing her yoga exercises out by the clothesline — she'd been inspired by the moon rising bloodred over the willow tree — he'd been dropping by with copies of The Watchtower, with its enthusiastic descriptions of what was going to happen to sinners when the apocalypse, which was always just around the corner, finally came.

It didn't really matter where we got the tree, because every year, no matter how scrawny or cockeyed, it was always the best we'd ever had. It might have been short in the woods, but in our living room, it stretched clear to the ceiling, laden with ornaments at least a jillion years old. There were photos of ancestors pasted into old Valentine cards, staring out of lacy birdcages and carriages and windows. There were swans hanging from little glass pendants, and angels that were actually pretty women cut from 1930s magazines and pasted onto cardboard.

All this gathered into a crescendo that landed on the dining room table in the form of night-before-Christmas dinner. After the seconds and thirds of turkey, mashed potatoes and giblet gravy, sauerkraut, Brussels sprouts, fruit salad, potato rolls, cranberry sauce and Aunt Stella's watermelon pickles, Dad would lean back from the turkey carcass and fake a stuporized exhaustion that was probably real.

"I think I'll go take a little nap," he'd say. "You wake me up before Santa gets here."

Then he'd stumble off upstairs, complaining that Santa never came when he was around. Shortly after that, the great Claus would sweep over our house, shouting to his reindeer, shaking his brass sleigh bells, rushing through our front door on a wave of polar air.

He looked so enormous standing there. And his eyes, as he bent down to look into ours, were a little bit scary.

"Why hello, little girl! My elves tell me you locked your sister in her room a while back!"

How did he know that? "Yeah, but we made up," I said nervously.

Santa In My Father's Shoes

"Where's that father of yours?" he'd growl. "Doesn't he care about Santa?"

We'd glance at each other nervously. Mother would explain how hard her husband had worked, putting up the tree.

"Oh! Kathleen! Well, it's always a pleasure to see you!" Santa would beam. Then he'd get a little kiss from Mom. We sensed why Santa liked to come when Dad was taking a nap.

We'd discuss the weather, maybe. How there was a blizzard over Philly. How Blitzen's leg was bothering him. How Grandmother had put on a few pounds. "Pot calling the kettle black?" she'd say.

Then Santa would reach into his great white laundry bag for our presents. One year he got his hand caught in a mousetrap "somebody" (my brother Jim shouted it was Dad) had placed in the bottom of his bag. Guess who didn't get a present that year.

One year he slipped on the little rug by the door, hurling himself to the floor with a house-shuddering crash.

"We've killed Santa," my sister said. Then he opened his eyes.

See why we believed? Until we were ready, we never connected those icy blue eyes, the bifocals and familiar shoes with our father. And none of us ever told our parents — or even each other — that we'd realized there was no Santa Claus. And so Santa continued to come every year, regardless of how old we were.

Until one year, when Dad was taken to the hospital with a ruptured appendix. He lay there, critically ill, hooked up to tubes and monitors.

The box containing Santa lay in the attic. It was really just some red flannel my mother had stitched together on her Singer, a fake beard and some bushy eyebrows my father had picked up years ago in a costume shop in Baltimore.

That year we just went through the motions. Jim played Santa, but it wasn't the same. We all kept thinking about the man in the hospital. We laughed too loud and our faces looked stiff. The rooms, usually so warm with light, all had hard edges.

In many ways, our real father was — and is — a hard man to get along with. He was often impatient, he yelled when he could have listened. But he was also full of stories and carried the same spark our Grandmother had, to make us tremble and laugh and later weave magic of our own.

He eventually recovered and played Santa for his grand-children. But there were other years, which seemed to multiply as we got older, when real life threatened to crack the surface of those happy rituals. I suppose that Linda Grady spoke the truth that day years ago. And I suppose that I recognized it in some cold center of my heart. But even then, I knew that there was too much truth like hers in the world, a kind of nay-saying dangerously close to death.

Nobody has to spell out reality for me. Our family has had its share of sadness, of bitter arguments that made empty places at the Christmas table.

And yet, sooner or later, we always seem to return, like a scattered band of foot soldiers, pulling into the farm in our old VW bugs and Volvos packed with kids and dogs, to take up our instruments and sing in a ragged but lusty chorus.

Anne Raver was Newsday's garden writer from 1986 through 1991. She was a feature writer, a books editor and a college teacher in Boston before coming to Newsday. She now writes about gardens and the environment for The New York Times. A collection of her essays, "Deep in the Green," was recently published. She gardens in Brooklyn.

A Joy That Comes With Time

by Amei Wallach

I meant to go into the woods and cut a Christmas tree this year. Cutting the tree was the only truly perfect part of my imperfect childhood Christmases. I can't remember when it started, when we first drove in my father's black De Soto that hated to start in the cold, to the home of Sumner Osgood, a minister who was one of his patients. I don't think I ever knew the denomination. It didn't seem to matter much.

What mattered were the trees — always two trees — we cut in his woods and dragged back to tie on the car, and then the kitchen with its ginger-bread smells and the hot chocolate and Rev. Osgood reading to us by the fireplace from "The Once and Future King," who, as it happened, was Arthur.

The friendly, spindly tree was for downstairs where we ate and watched television. It got fat colored lights and toy decorations and the marzipan wreaths for which my mother each year made the three-hour pilgrimage in sleet and snow from northwestern Connecticut to Elk Candy Company on 86th Street in Manhattan. The big, lush tree was for upstairs in our living room, where my father, with a great deal of frustration and drama, made his stained glass windows out of cellophane, because stained glass reminded him of his boyhood and the cathedral in Cologne. That was the show tree, strictly blue and silver bulbs, masses of cotton-like snow on the branches, and boxes of tinsel hung thickly, strand by persnickety strand. And, of course, the candles.

The candles on the tree were a cause for awe and anxiety in the neighborhood. Everyone was sure that one Christmas the house would burn down. My mother still lights real candles on her tree, as she did in Germany, and we still gather nervously about, snuffing them as they grow short, while my mother blithely hawks her plates of cookies. "Here, you have to try this one. Don't you like my cookies this year?"

It would be Christmas Eve when the candles were lit. I still wore pigtails for the ones I remember best. My mother was always having to comb the snarls out to braid them; I was always yelling; we were always late.

My little brother, Bunny, was still young enough to relish, if not precisely believe, the idea of Santa in the days of my pigtails. We called him Bunny because he was born on Easter, though his name was Wendell after (Republican) Willkie as my middle name was Eleanor after (Democrat) Roosevelt in an immigrant's eager attempt at political evenhandedness. My older brother was really

Hans Gert Max Klaus Peter after my father, but the Peter part seemed more American, so that was the part that stuck.

Peter is a professor now. And it was he who told me, with exactness of detail, the truth about Santa Claus. That in no way, however, dimmed the delights of the family friend who dressed as Santa each Christmas Eve, with Bunny as her elf. It was Santa and Bunny who would light the tree, and then jingle their bells and "Ho, ho, ho," to signal the time had come to enter the Christmas room.

Which was hushed, and waiting in the glow of the candles. Before anything else happened, I sat down at the Steinway and hacked out Christmas carols, and Bunny blew his clarinet, and Peter read a prayer he had written, and we all sang "Silent Night" in German, and the time had come for present-opening. It wasn't the presents that counted, though. Or the anticipation of their opening that I've tried to recapture ever since. It was the hush of ceremony. Particularly since it was bracketed at each end with what happened when the tree wouldn't stand straight, which it never would, or my mother's Christmas stollen was too hard to eat, or the telephone rang at midnight and my father had to go out in the snow. It mattered so much for it all to be perfect; it was so easy for something to go wrong. It was so easy for catastrophe to strike. For Roxy, the dog-of-mixed-blood, to bark in bereavement and longing and my mother to erupt in outrage because once again we children had forgotten to fill the dog's dish. For me to run wailing to my room because someone had dared to criticize my lapse. For my father to break into a litany of German swear words he could manage for minutes at a time without taking a breath, because once again everything was noisy and at odds and not as it ought to be.

I don't know how much the unquietness had to do with the fact that it was Christmas and we were Jewish. It was because they were Jewish that my parents had left Germany. In Germany, my mother's beloved governess, Welle, was Protestant. She took the chil-

A Joy That Comes With Time

dren to little Lutheran churches on the moors. My mother remembered those churches in the rain; she'd stand under the eaves and feel embraced. Synagogue was for special occasions with the parents, for dress-up and no misbehaving. In Germany there had been a Christmas tree at my grandmother's, two stories high, and guests in diamonds and satin to revel around it while the children peered down from the upstairs banister. The guests, too, kept Christmas trees at home, and synagogue for special occasions.

In this new world of New England, my father became a Methodist, and my mother was a Quaker. In summer, she took us to family camps where the young men wore hair on their faces and no shoes on their feet. They spoke of Christ and of conscience, and went to prison because they would not sign up to be drafted. In winter, at church, I was an angel at the crèche, with my hair loose and long and a candle in my hands. "Christ the Savior is bo-orn," I sang as later we would sing 'round the Christmas tree. "Christ the savior is born!"

Too many years of my adulthood have been spent trying to re-create the perfect Christmas that never was. My husband, on the other hand, who had once been a Catholic, had a great many secret reasons to despise the Christmases of his boyhood. In his family they gave checks at Christmas, though there was a tree, and too much, too good apple pie. There was also mass, though he never spoke of that. To him it was all forced merriness, forced gift-giving. His favorite gift from me was the tie with Bah Humbug repeated on it 200 times. By the time I knew enough to give it to him, it was too late. The Christmases in between were battlegrounds. I wanted a big tree to trim, big logs in the fireplace, big emotions, a big family gathering around a table set in white with my mother's blue plates from Dresden and red candles. His perfect Christmas would have been for it all to go away.

In the five years since my divorce, I've rather finessed Christmas. I thought I was being adult about it. Accepting what was instead of yearning for something that couldn't be. I no longer wanted to make someone do Christmas my way. At first it was a feverish round of friends who felt like strangers, now that I was one, not two, and unaccustomed to myself. That was the time of elegant Christmas dinners in the bosom of other people's families.

Then one year, I tried for the hush. The family came down from New England in 60-degree weather. On Christmas Eve, we walked across Central Park in spring mud to St. Luke's Church because the music was supposed to be wonderful there. But it was efficient, and empty of promise. We saw "Gandhi" the next day, though, and found a hush, after all. But even that year I didn't have a tree, just red cyclamen in a white basket.

Since then, it's been Christmas Eve at Bunny's in Connecticut. We've sung "Stille Nacht" and feasted at his groaning board of vegetable delicacies. The next day, those of us with a craving for meat might take Christmas dinner at Peter's.

We — my mother, my brothers, their families and I — had learned the lessons of accommodation. Christmas became a time for wrapping last-minute presents together, for companionability, for eating too much marzipan and helping with the dishes. Perhaps it lacked a little in ritual and in old ways that seemed mistily far away. But there was a sort of peace in that. Somewhere along the way I went to Israel. I wept at the Wailing Wall and on the Via Dolorosa. They didn't seem like contradictions. I am Jewish, but I was raised a Christian.

And somewhere along the way I've accumulated my own, new traditions. My friend Rosamund Morley plays vielle with the Waverly Consort. Last year I went to hear her at The Cloisters and held her 5-month-old daughter, Katharine, on my knee. Katharine was too squirmy for The Cloisters this year, but I was there, anyway, with my new friend, Bill, after onion tart and too much wine, and the sun on the Hudson River. And there was magic to the music.

A Joy That Comes With Time

Bill is crazy about Christmas. He has so many decorations, each with its own story from Christmases past, that he offered to share the overflow. But he'd put me in the way of the Christmas spirit and already I'd bought Chinese straw fishes from the Museum of Natural History and Taiwanese wooden pigs from the Village. Because this year I have a tree. It's three feet high and cost $30, and there's hardly room for the 200 lights I grabbed before they were all gone at the Five & Ten. In the end there wasn't time to drive two hours each way to go into the woods and cut a tree. We took Bill's 19-year-old daughter, Kate, to brunch at the Russian Tea Room instead. Somehow that meant more than recapturing slippery memories.

Bill fills his place with music every day. Mozart, the Boss and Jackson Browne. It tickles him no end that I'd never heard of Jackson Browne. He reads me T.S. Eliot when we hike, and Garrison Keillor when we don't. He'll spend 20 minutes on the phone with his son, Tony, in Minneapolis, explaining step-by-step with joy and humor how to tie a tie. He'll take a morning to succor an acquaintance who's out of a job, or spend all afternoon hooking up my rickety stereo to the speakers he's lent me so we can indulge in "Graceland" and the German Christmas carols he's recorded. Then it's he who goes out in the cold to move the car. Lately, we've been playing the "Messiah" a lot so we can go somewhere and sing along.

He knows all the words already.

This will be Bill's first Christmas Eve without his children. But with all those old memories. We'll go to midnight services after Bunny's. Maybe I'll read something. It could be from "The Once and Future King," but it doesn't have to be. We'll make this Christmas ours. New and for the first time. Not perfect. A little frayed at the edges maybe, but joyful. Like the "Messiah" sing-in, with its untrained enthusiasms, its surfeit of good-will and good fellowship and raggedy harmonies and rhythms. We'll take pleasure in improvising as we go along.

My mother's card this year comes from the Fellowship of Reconciliation. "Expect a miracle," it says on the front between the flippers of Jonah's whale. "Shalom!" it says, on the inside.

"I chose it because I'm neither fish nor fowl," my mother told me when I asked. "And somehow it struck a chord."

The girl with the pigtails, who could wail as soon as carol, may have wanted a perfect Christmas. But Christmas is messier and more enchanting than that.

Christmas is about ancient wisdoms. It is about family memories and family myths, about forgiven family lies and tarnished family promises. But most of all, Christmas is about love, and it is about renewal. It celebrates a birth.

Amei Wallach, born in New York City, was Newsday's art critic for many years. She also was an on-air arts essayist for the "MacNeil / Lehrer NewsHour." Her book on Russian artist Ilya Kabakov was recently published. She contributes to many magazines, including Vanity Fair, Vogue and Architectural Digest.

by Roy Hanson

Years ago, on Christmas Eve, in newspaper city rooms, the wire service machines, which spent 363 days and 18 hours chattering out news, would spend six hours sending something different.

The Teletype operators in bureaus all over the world — AP in London, UP (not UPI, then) in Tokyo, INS in Paris (International News Service survives only like the Cheshire Cat's grin, as the I in UPI) — would send Christmas cards.

And elaborate cards they were, drawn in capital letters of the alphabet — forests of Christmas trees, shepherds and seraphim, mangers and Magi, and cathedrals with bells.

You could see them form, line by line, sometimes letter by letter if it was to be, say, a spire. And you could try to guess what was to be. I'd like to think, in retrospect, that it was a way

Christmas
In The Loose-Knit Swamp

Christmas In The Loose-Knit Swamp

for a teletype operator, anonymous all year, to say, "I'm a person and so are we all, and Merry Christmas." But it was mostly just a way for them to show off, of course.

The cards would have been fun for kids, but there were no kids in the city rooms, only serious, grown-up people, watching seriously for important news. It never came on Christmas Eve. At least not to me. At least not that kind.

I suppose you could say that the news that came on Christmas Eve almost 2,000 years ago was so important that there hasn't been any news on Christmas Eve since.

The wire service machines would issue their Christmas cards onto the floor behind them. And the wire editor would slice them off with his ruler, neatly, one at a time. Not because he wanted to preserve them; that was the way he removed stories from the machine, so he did the Christmas cards the same way.

Sometimes he would take one that he thought was particularly nice out of the wire room to show to the copy desk, which had, collectively, just about finished with all the news it wanted to deal with (and had to) and was, collectively, sipping Scotch out of paper cups.

Henry Grabowski would look at the wire service Christmas card and say, "Very nice, very nice," but he did not sound sincere.

Then he would say, "What a loose-knit swamp this is."

He always said that.

And Maurice Gerard, the slot man, would ask to see the card, and he would look at it very carefully, with one eye closed, and eventually pronounce it a masterpiece. He was undoubtedly sincere, although probably out of focus.

Gerard had never married. Nor had Rick Johnson, there on the far corner of the desk. At least as far as anybody knew. Rick would sometimes talk about the places he'd been since graduating Harvard some 40 years before, but he never indicated that anybody had been there with him. Rick had started celebrating Christmas in October, right around the time he stopped celebrating Labor Day.

Harry Meyer had worked as many places as Rick. And we believed him. He'd had big jobs on big papers, but he'd returned to this town in his 60s because it was his wife's birthplace. He rode home to her every morning about 4 on one of the newspaper's delivery trucks.

Dave Naylor had a wife, and a girlfriend, and seemed equally devoted to both. Or to neither.

The wire editor was younger than the others by, in most cases, 30 years or so. At the beginning of that year the wire editor was a man named John O'Keefe. John, who was in his early 60s, died of a heart attack in the spring. Then Bob Stewart, who was about the same age, was made wire editor. And he had a heart attack one night in the midst of editing the lead story, and he died. The new wire editor was 26. He figured he had been given the job based mostly on life expectancy. O'Keefe and Stewart were the real names of those two men; the other names in this story are fictitious ones, although the people are real.

None of them seemed to mind working on Christmas Eve. At least as long as the Scotch held out. And it always did. They were provident in at least that regard if no other.

If any of them felt they were there for any higher purpose, they never said.

It was easier, though, in those days, to think that the newspaper business was special. Childish ways, but . . .

The wire editor, for instance, did know things that were not known to other people. When the wires finally went back into the news-grinding business, for instance, sometime after midnight, on Christmas Day, they would probably say this:

BETHLEHEM (AP) — A TENSE CALM REIGNED OVER CHRIST'S BIRTHPLACE TODAY AS PILGRIMS . . .

Christmas In The Loose-Knit Swamp

They said that every Christmas.

And for a while, the wire editor would have this information all to himself, for what it was worth. Not that even the wire editor, young as he was, was overwhelmed at possessing the knowledge of Bethlehem's tense calmness. Or calm tenseness. No, it was always a tense calm, not a calm tension.

Now, a newspaper city room is one of the last places in the world you would want to be if you wanted to know what's going on. The best place to be is home watching the Cable News Network.

But the Bethlehem story wouldn't move until later. On this Christmas Eve, the bureaus were still sending Christmas cards. An elaborate snowflake from Rome, a cathedral built of the letter T, over and over, from Paris. There were still exotic places in the world. Now we think we know them because we've seen them on television. Like Narcissus, we've fallen in love with a reflection of the world.

It was certainly harder to communicate when you had to build your message a tiny brick at a time like this:

```
      M         M
M   M   M       M
M    M M        M
M     M         M
```

Until you had spelled out Merry Christmas.

On the copy desk, Maurice was trying to keep Rick sober by feeding him black coffee from the restaurant downstairs. Rick was spiking the coffee from the Scotch bottle. Dave Naylor was on the phone murmuring Merry Christmases. To someone. Better to work on Christmas Eve than to have someone know you're somewhere else. Harry Meyer was reading advance society page copy and grumbling because all brides carried stephanotis. And every once in a while

Henry Grabowski would cry, "Merry Christmas," and add, "What a loose-knit swamp this is!"

The wire editor walked back and forth from his seat on the copy desk to the wire room, to see if anything had happened. There would still be time to get something in the paper. But the wires moved nothing but Christmas cards, from New York, Chicago, Boston, San Francisco. Sleighs and snowmen and candy canes. Built by anonymous hands, appearing letter by letter all over the country.

There was a particularly nice Christmas card from UP's Paris Bureau. A cathedral — it might have been meant to be Notre Dame, although the wire editor wouldn't recognize Notre Dame without a hunchback on it. Whatever it was, it was very elaborate and impressive. He thought about showing it to somebody, but decided not to.

Dave Naylor had finished his phone call — or were there two? Maurice had given up on feeding Rick coffee and they were both drinking the Scotch. "The bride," intoned Harry Meyer, "carried lilies and stephanotis . . . I'm going to change that to poinsettia."

Harry died the following spring.

And Maurice is dead now, and Rick, since years have passed. Dave Naylor, who was younger than most of the others then, is still alive, as are his girlfriend and his wife. And Henry Grabowski, the last I heard. He's retired long since. I hope he travels, and when he arrives — wherever it is — looks around with scorn and says, "What a loose-knit swamp this is." I sometimes picture him in the Everglades.

At about 2 a.m., the AP wire moved its first story in hours . . . about a particularly bad car crash in Pittsburgh. It would never have made the national wire any other night. The wire editor had been betting with himself that the first story would be the one saying Bethlehem was calm, although tense. So he was wrong. That was the second story.

Christmas In The Loose-Knit Swamp

Henry Grabowski wound a scarf around his neck again and again like an elderly Hans Brinker, observed for the final time what a loose-knit swamp this was, said Merry Christmas and headed home. Dave Naylor left, heading somewhere. Maurice and Rick trilled Merry Christmases all the way to the door — each one of them supporting the other, or so he seemed to think. Harry Meyer remained behind; the newspaper delivery truck wouldn't leave for another two hours.

In the wire room, the wire editor gathered up the Christmas cards and dumped them into a wastebasket.

* * *

The wire services don't send those Christmas cards any more. The copy moves on VDT screens now, and there are no Teletype operators to draw the pictures. And the wire editor is older, too, and has seen more Christmas Eves, in other places.

That is, I have. It seemed more appropriate to refer to the wire editor in the third person (it does seem so long ago). But it was me. And, as I said, I've spent other Christmas Eves, with strangers and with loved ones. In my own home and at other people's, in churches and in barrooms and in places even looser-knit.

And of course I've received a lot of Christmas cards over the years — and I appreciate them more as the years go by.

But I still wish I'd saved at least one of those wire service creations. A simple one, perhaps, spelling out in an assemblage of capital letters: Merry Christmas. Or even, "What a loose-knit swamp this is."

Roy Hanson was a writer and an editor at Newsday for 27 years. A native of Connecticut, he spent three years as a paratrooper in the U.S. Army's 82nd Airborne Division. His series of articles on living with cancer won him awards and great praise. He died in 1989.

Undimmed Spirit In An Ugly Time

by Marilyn Milloy

Some months ago, long before most folks' fancy turned to this matter of Christmas, my sister and I sat in our pajamas in a sunny corner of her Tennessee house, clutching big, fat pillows as we giggled like schoolgirls about little else but, well, Christmas.

We'd actually awakened that crisp Chattanooga morning bent on planning a rare holiday trip home together to Shreveport,

Undimmed Spirit In An Ugly Time

La. But to observe us — grown women rolling on the floor at the mere mention of Glover's Mange, the putrid shampoo our mother used every Christmas Eve to wash our hair — was to know we really were not planning a trip at all, but doing our perennial "remember when" routine.

"Remember red light, green light?" Docia whispered with a smirk and an expectant stare.

"With the Christmas tree color wheel!" I howled knowingly. And we were off — she to muse about how nary a Christmas seemed to go by without our playing that raucous hiding game with our big brother, me to recall how I always ended up the loser, getting caught by the color wheel every time it turned the tree red. "Fools we were," Docia said finally, snickering at the thought of it all. "Fools," said I, following suit.

And on it went. Like it always does. Same holiday memories. Same laughs.

I long ago stopped trying to figure out why my sister, my brother and I indulge year after year in those same old memories, on occasion even engaging our weary spouses and friends.

There really was nothing to figure out.

We relished those family Christmases at the time, and through no real mystery, we relish thinking of them now. In our minds, no child's holidays could have been more magical, so spirited was the atmosphere in our little Poland Street house, so absolute, and embarrassingly long-lasting, was our belief in Mr. Claus, his elves, sugarplum fairies, the goodness of humankind even.

What amazes me, still, is how our parents, a black man and woman raising three children in a hostile and segregated South, could so "fix" these things to be our tender memories.

Not all of it is a mystery. My parents were schoolteachers — advantaged, on our side of the tracks — and able to grant childhood wishes that somehow masked for us the brutal inequities of the day. Thus, in various years I did get the Little Miss Echo doll I so desperately wanted, and the EasyBake oven and the skates with the key. And one year, when my daddy, a skilled photographer, got extra work taking wedding pictures, I got a bicycle with training wheels.

These gifts were deeply satisfying and were the impetus behind many an unfinished thank-you note to Santa. Yet far more basic to those utterly "normal" Christmases, in utterly disturbing times, was my parents' unshakable belief in protecting the innocence of our childhood. They not only insisted on embellishing that wonderful myth about the deliverer of our holiday treasures, but on creating for us a world where dreams went unencumbered, where tomorrows were awaited with excitement and wonder, and where, as a result of all that, self-assurance flourished.

In our protected house, the stench of racial hatred did not penetrate. Attitudes about black inferiority were miraculously shooed to distant places by these guardians of happiness. Instilled naïveté was our shield against the reality of our "colored" status, which was everywhere beyond our doorstep. We did have to sit in the balcony of the movie house on the rare occasions we went there, and on the back seats of the trolleys when we rode them. This was just the way the world was. People basically were good, and so, too, were we to be. "God don't like ugly," we were told, and this we seriously took to heart.

Great effort went into creating this world of ours. It is difficult to fathom otherwise how my father — whose own father was shot dead by a white man in his Arkansas hometown because of a vicious rumor that a white woman had visited him — not only avoided telling us of this travesty until we were near adulthood, but avoided, despite his outrage, a single venomous outburst about white people in our wide-eyed presence. Or how my mother, who had picked cotton on a South Carolina farm, managed for years to let on not even a detail of the gutter poverty of her youth or the never-to-be-forgotten humiliation by whites that made it all the more bitter.

Undimmed Spirit In An Ugly Time

It was not until long past our Santa days that she even confided how she'd visit the department stores during Christmastime and stand quietly in a corner. There she'd scope out the various white Santa Clauses on their thrones to determine, I suppose in ways only mothers know, which one was more likely than not to insult her babies. Similarly, long before we stepped foot with her in any store, she would confirm that, yes, they would let us try on hats there, or the "can-can" underskirts for our Christmas dresses.

So accustomed were we to this insulation that, on the occasion the stench of racism did waft so close that we stole a whiff, we were puzzled. When blacks in Shreveport boycotted the state fair when it reserved a special visiting day for us, we knew something was wrong. And when, against my father's judgment, my mother marched us into a hamburger joint one lazy afternoon and was politely refused an order of take-out ice cream cones, we definitely sensed this was not how it was supposed to be.

But these events were so isolated, so fleeting — and so skillfully dismissed for us by our parents — that the magnitude of the racial problem never quite rocked us until our teenage years, when our fragile sensibilities had toughened and we were comfortable with, and irreversibly proud of, who we were. By then there seemed no insult we could not handle, no issue we could not confront, at least with a little help from our folks.

And that's where those early Christmas holidays came in. For it was those times, perhaps more than any others, when the community that swaddled us seemed at its best, when our own family seemed, by our lights, at its best, as well.

At every turn during those days there were things to look forward to and be a part of. There were the Christmas canned food drives at school, which I got a kick out of since there was always the chance I might get to help haul our homeroom bounty to the auditorium for sorting. This, for some reason, was made by our teachers to seem like an honor and a very big privilege.

There was the pulling of names for the purpose of gift-giving, an exercise which never got started without a teacher's lecture about how awful and selfish and ugly we would look if we held our nose at the name we got. EVERYBODY, they'd always say, deserves a treat, and for me this was good to hear, given the not-so-fond feelings I had for a boy named Marty, who yanked my ponytails, followed me home from school and could have me awash in tears without even being around.

Finally, there were the church plays, in which everybody who ever showed their faces in a Sunday school class managed to have a role. Twice I played an angel and my brother Courtland was a wise man. But my sister's dream of being Mary always eluded her.

She seemed destined to animal roles — a donkey one year, a lamb another. Still, we always went home beaming, what with the standing ovations, the hugs from Rev. Scott and what seemed the ultimate token: a much-anticipated brown paper bag filled with apples, oranges, brazil nuts and hard red candy, the pieces of which we'd dutifully count on the way home to see which among us was "ahead."

At home the excitement came accompanied with chores we hardly ever protested doing. Each year we helped our mother get the house spotless before we lifted from the boxes the white flocked tree, the red Christmas balls, the plastic silver star and that squeaky color wheel.

Daddy dug out his ladder and we helped him string lights across the house, onto this bush, that tree. Then at night we'd all pile in the car and he'd drive what seemed miles to the white part of town, where the rich people lived. There we'd gaze with wonder upon beautifully lit mansion-sized houses with leaping reindeer out front and giant nativity scenes, and argue passionately over which one was "mine."

Christmas Eve we were down to business. Mom washed our hair with Glover's Mange so Santa would smell fresh heads when

Undimmed Spirit In An Ugly Time

he tiptoed in to kiss them. I'd finish any reminders I needed to write to our red–suited visitor, and my sister and I would bake cookies to set out with the milk while Mom began our holiday dinner, which we often ate with neighbors. With the smell of chocolate chips still in the air and Nat King Cole on the record player, we were then tucked into "fresh" beds, wearing "fresh" pajamas, and ordered to go to sleep.

It is perhaps not much worth telling about the obvious thrill of the morning when it came. Suffice it to say that the magic has lasted — not so much the element of surprise that attends many Christmases, what with the gift–giving and all, but the overall special-ness of the season, its ability to infuse families and communities with a good and hopeful spirit.

The way I figure, even if our parents had not orchestrated these rituals and shielded us from ugliness and celebrated our youth, I think I still would be looking forward to the warmth of the holiday.

But I think the feeling could never quite be what it is now, for what makes my heart tingle these days is not just things like love and birth so embodied in the celebration called Christmas, but the determination of our parents during difficult and humiliating times to make our lives a joy.

And so when we all sit down at the table on Christmas Day, this family of mine, we will raise at least two apple cider toasts. One will be to this special time together again.

The other will be to our mom and dad.

Marilyn Milloy *was a writer for Newsday from 1982 through 1995. She reported from the Washington bureau and was the paper's Atlanta bureau chief. She is currently free-lancing.*

Family Trees

by Lynn Darling

At my mother's house, there are always two Christmas trees.

The one in the living room is the formal tree, a '50s dream of peace on Earth or, at least, contentment in the suburbs. It's usually a tall elegant spruce hung with delicate glass ornaments, many faded now with age, translucent in their fragility. Each branch shimmers with carefully placed tinsel, draped strand by strand. The tinsel, too, is old, packed up each year by my mother, who considers it a sin to throw anything away. The base is covered in snowy white cotton, plumped into hills and valleys by crumpled newspaper underneath. Nestled into the folds are the landmarks of a small plastic town: pharmacy, post office, airport control tower. Christmas in Levittown, perhaps, but not a bad mock-up of the suburbs of my childhood. All of the lights are blue, because blue is my father's favorite color.

The angel on top arrived when I

did: My parents liked to identify me with her, though that became less easy as I got older. It is a tree rich in our family's history; memories hang heavy on the branches.

We never sit beneath that tree on Christmas morning.

The other tree appeared for the first time about 10 or 15 years ago; my parents had moved yet again, and a fancier house in a fancier neighborhood demanded a second tree. The result materialized in the family room: a small, bushy tree festooned with plaid ribbons and shiny papier-mâché apples and lifelike plump songbirds. It's anybody's tree, and it's nobody's tree, a glossy reminder of nothing, a tree that has as much to do with our past as Ralph Lauren does with true Americana.

But because it stands in the family room, where we congregate when we are not in the kitchen, it has become the real tree: the one we put our presents under, the one surrounded late Christmas morning by torn wrapping paper and half-empty coffee cups and brand-new sweaters, the usual detritus of the day.

For a long time now, it has made me crazy that we do this, that we ignore our history in the living room and gather before a designer tree, because while this is partly due to convenience, it also says much about my family, about the immaculate way we have shed our past, making ourselves up as we go along.

It was a not unusual story in a restless postwar '50s America: My father, a young man from a New England farming family, joined the Army as a way up and out; my mother, the daughter of Polish immigrants, left her large and boisterous family behind in Pittsburgh to follow him across the country and around the world. We grew up, my two brothers and I, by creating ourselves anew in each community we landed in, learning to fit into the prevailing flora and fauna without ever putting out any roots.

We did this awkwardly, trying on personalities over identities that had not yet gelled. We were practiced at the art of camou-

flage; it was the '50s, we lived in a swoon of conformity. Or at least we tried. My mother had other ideas. She tried to graft her deeply old-fashioned notions of domesticity and her very Slavic sense of emotion onto the shaky little sapling of our life in the suburbs. I was deeply embarrassed that she baked her own bread instead of buying it in a plastic wrapper, that she made homemade potato chips for our birthday parties, even by the rage of her desire to bring her family up in the world: Her laughter and her anger were storms that blew apart the placid propriety of the other mothers.

We didn't see much of my mother's family when we were growing up, but when we did, I noticed only the way in which they differed from my idea of normal families. I blushed to see my grandmother sitting outside our front door on soft summer evenings, her stockings rolled down to just below her knees, her voice, roughened by years of living life on its harshest terms, ringing out over the smooth square lawns and slamming into the curtained windows and darkened doors of our neighbors. I cringed at Polish jokes, worried that they contained some truth I could not escape. I wanted no part of my heritage. I wanted only to be invisible.

But in the '60s, in college, where the worst sin was to be "white bread," a bland member of the oppressor class, I suddenly became Polish. I talked proudly of my steelworker grandfather and tossed the few words of Polish I knew into every conversation, whether they were appropriate or not. I plied my grandmother for quaint tales of the old days in the old country. My grandmother, fierce and flinty, looked at me like I was crazy. "Why would anyone want to remember?" she said. "Why would anyone want to talk about what was so terrible?"

But I wasn't Polish, any more than I was genteel WASP suburban. I had no roots, I decided, I came from nowhere. I tried to make this glamorous when I was young; I saw myself as a woman of mystery. But as I grew older, the lack of connection was more lonely, more unsettling. There was no hometown to use as a measure of how far I'd come, no culture to harken back to, no heirlooms burnished by twicetold tales of the heroes and heroines of generations past. We were newly hatched; we had measured our rise in the world by how well we blended in, and there was nothing to mark our place.

Christmas etched the contradictions more sharply, particularly when I was in my 20s, an arrogant age. I was no more connected to my family than I was to my past. Our family was splintered by the ideological rifts of the '60s, and also by the very different life into which my parents had educated me — they had worked hard to give me something better, only to lose me to a different culture, a different set of values. I must have been insufferable, wrapped in my hip liberal urbanity, threatened by a togetherness when I was still trying to establish my autonomy, a fledgling sense of self. I had no idea how to mesh the adult I had become with the child I once was.

Eventually, things got a little better — I forgave my parents for the crime of not being perfect, but I gave up on Christmas. It was only a frozen awkward ritual, to be gotten through and then forgotten. If Christmas was about anything, it seemed to me, it was about an unhesitating, trusting, unconditional love that I no longer felt capable of giving, and a sense of wonder I was too jaded to entertain. I had spent too much time, I told myself, shoring up the defenses, keeping an eye on the escape hatches, limiting the risk. I had spent too much time trying on images to know who I was in relation to all these people, these people who were meant to be my family.

And then, this year, I had a baby.

My mother came up to help me those first few sleepless weeks. I was an abject trembling version of my formal self, my carefully plotted life exploded into starry little fragments. I was overwhelmed with joy and tears, terrified of my own incompetence.

It was my mother who pulled me through.

Caring for my daughter brought back her memories of my own infancy, and together we pored through the big red family photograph albums in the quiet blurry hours late at night while the bassinet trembled with the tiny movements of a restless little creature still dreaming of a safe dark place. I looked at the pictures with new eyes. I saw myself at my daughter's age, I thought of the woman my daughter would become. I looked at the pictures of a beautiful young woman and a handsome young man starting a life together and for the first time felt their youth and saw their dreams without making the vengeful tallies of what those dreams had cost me. Painfully, passionately, I learned about wonder and began to understand about love.

My mother began to tell me stories, about those long-ago days, when she was a young military wife — about the white-glove inspections of her housekeeping and her terror of the older officers' wives, of laundry freezing on the line in a Kansas winter, of the struggle to get by as she tried to learn the rules of a rigid hierarchy. I saw the woman she was before the mother she became, I saw her for herself at last, without the veil of authority and power that had always obscured her.

My mother brought my 85-year-old grandmother to see my daughter. My grandmother watched the baby she would never know and who would never know her, watched her avidly, as if trying to discern the life my daughter had ahead of her. Maybe that's why, as we sat around the table one morning drinking coffee, she began at last to tell her own stories.

They were not the cozy tales I had once begged her for. She talked about what it was like to be one of 12 children, born to a coal miner and his wife, of how desperately poor they were, how her father beat them and drank his paycheck away. Stories of how she ran away at the age of 15 to the big city of Pittsburgh and went to work in a department store, washing dishes in the lunchroom there, and her wonder at the snowy white tablecloths and sparkling glassware and the furs that the ladies wore. And she wept as she described her mother's love for the man who finally abandoned her, and the tears raced down

Family Trees

the deep creases carved in her old and angry face.

     I thought of the baby in the white bassinet and the young girl in a Pennsylvania coal mining town and of all the ways in which the world of my grandmother had formed my mother, had formed me and would now become a part of my daughter. I was connected, after all. I understood who we were — not in terms of dusty rituals and the formal portraits of distinguished ancestors, but in the light of the dreams we had lived by and the nightmares, in the hopes and fears that had guided the choices we had made and shaped the people we had become, our strengths and our weaknesses.

     Recently my mother came back for a visit, and one evening she looked through the album once again, hoping to trace the similarities between my now 10-month-old daughter and myself at that age,

when my father saw me for the first time, when we joined him in Tokyo at the end of the Korean War. A few pages forward, she stopped at a picture of me on my first Christmas, posed before a tree that bore the first several of the ornaments that now crowd the lonely tree in my parents' living room. "You know, we never had a tree when I was growing up," she said. "We didn't have the money."

     So I go home this Christmas to the house with two trees with my husband and my daughter, and I will leave behind my chilly disdain for a newly minted custom that had its origins in a yearning long ago. The trees are part of our family, they are who we are — tradition is not only a matter of the things we do pass on, but of the hungers we no longer have to.

Lynn Darling was a feature writer for Newsday from 1986 to 1993, after eight years of writing for The Washington Post's Style section. She is now a senior writer at Esquire magazine.

The Year Of The Bride Doll

by Sheryl McCarthy

It was the Christmas of my ninth or tenth year. I don't remember exactly, except that it was the Christmas I got Cindy, my bride doll.

She was waiting there under the tree when I emerged from my bedroom on Christmas morning, wide awake after a feverish night of insomnia brought on by my anticipation of Christmas Day. She wore a white satin dress trimmed in lace, and a veil trailed from her bobbed hair. She had red lips, dark brown eyes and a face that was pretty yet seemed more intelligent than those of most other dolls. She was black, too, a deep brown color, the richness of which still surprises me when I look at her now.

The Year Of The Bride Doll

As with all the Christmases that preceded this one, the cherished doll was the most highly prized of my new toys. And it was her arrival that prompted my mother to exclaim: "Oh, let's have a wedding!"

To understand the significance of the doll wedding, you must understand the special place that dolls occupied in my growing up. Since as far back as I can remember, I always got a new doll for Christmas. And that doll became for me the centerpiece of the day. The very first one was Yvette, who arrived when I was a year old. I don't remember that Christmas at all, or getting the doll, but I have Yvette to this day. She sits on top of a bookshelf in my old bedroom in my parents' house. She wears her original blue satin dress trimmed with ruffles. The material is delicate, worn thin by washings over the years. She wears a matching bonnet over black hair that has lost most of its curl. Her lips are red and two "real teeth" are in her slightly opened mouth. The teeth are somewhat recessed, having been knocked back from years of handling. Like Cindy, Yvette is also black, one of the few black dolls in my collection. When I was growing up, in the '50s and '60s, there weren't very many black dolls, so she and Cindy are unique. Yvette is also special because she is my oldest doll and the one that bears my middle name.

I have always been fascinated with dolls. I get this from my mother, who, I suppose, may have longed for fancy dolls when she was growing up during the Depression. I know choosing a new doll for me each Christmas seemed to delight her as much as getting them did me. I don't remember the names of most of my dolls, and there were so many of them that even their faces are a blur. I know there was the three-foot-high walking doll with the long blond hair; a very French-looking doll with porcelain skin who wore a stylish dress and an upswept hairdo; and there were Barbie and Ken and their pals, including a fluffy pet poodle. Barbie and the others were my last dolls, acquired when I was 13 and starting to be too old for such childish amusements.

Until then, however, each Christmas I carried my new doll around with me to the homes of my girlfriends. They showed me their toys, and I showed off my latest doll. I took very good care of my doll children. Some girls are obsessed with combing and brushing their dolls' hair, which means that a month after Christmas their poor dolls are half bald and missing their underpants, a shoe or sock and a few buttons from the harsh treatment to which their owners had subjected them. But my dolls never looked like orphans. Not wanting to disrupt their carefully set hairstyles, I refrained from combing my dolls' hair. I also knew that dust was an enemy of dolls' hair. If it accumulated, it made the synthetic hair dry and dull. I remember blowing the dust off my dolls' heads regularly, and as a result even these many years later their hair retains most of the original gloss and shape. Nor did any of my dolls get thrown away. I still have 20 or so of them, and they look pretty much the same as when I was a kid. Most of them sit around my old bedroom, while others are packed away in closets.

Once, when I returned home from college, I noticed that a couple of my dolls looked a little beat-up. It seems my grandmother had allowed the little girl next door to play with them in my absence, and the child had not treated the dolls well. I was not pleased. I believe dolls should be handled gently, like delicate children.

Anyway, that particular Christmas my mother came up with the idea of having a doll wedding. As she described her vision of it, I became as excited as she. We'd hold a wedding ceremony and have Cindy married properly, and we'd invite all my girlfriends to the event. Once the idea was hatched, plans for the wedding proceeded at a feverish pace. The first obstacle was to find Cindy a suitable groom. I owned no boy dolls, and the closest thing I had to one was a Howdy Doody hand puppet. The problem was, being a hand puppet, Howdy had no legs. I guess you could say it was like taking a man with rough edges but plenty of potential and molding him into husband material.

The Year Of The Bride Doll

Using stuff we had around the house — maybe it was some empty paper towel rolls — my mother fashioned some legs for Howdy and dressed him in a little tuxedo she had sewn. When we got through with him, the red-haired, freckled Mr. Doody cut a dashing figure as the groom.

There were dresses to be made for the bridesmaids, which were chosen from among my stable of dolls. My mother sewed these dresses herself, and I believe there were three or four bridesmaids. Invitations went out to my cadre of girlfriends. On the appointed day, the wedding took place in the den of our house. With my friends sitting around in their dressy dresses, wearing braids and ribbons or with their hair done up in holiday curls, they sat around the den, waiting for the wedding to begin.

It started with my mother's playing "Here Comes the Bride" on the piano. I marched the dolls into the room — first the bridesmaids, then Howdy Doody in his tuxedo and finally Cindy, who was a radiant and serene bride. I can't recall who conducted the marriage ceremony, but I know that in my role as the mother of the bride, who was losing a daughter (and gaining only a hand puppet for a son-in-law), I sobbed loudly throughout the ceremony. Afterwards I collected myself, and my friends and I feasted on cake and other goodies my mother had prepared for the reception.

In the panoply of events that made up my childhood, the doll wedding stands out as one of the most magical. To begin with, it was fun. It was a chance to put on a show, to act out an adult spectacle on a small scale. Second, and immensely important for a pre-adolescent, it impressed my friends, who had never seen such a thing and who would never have thought of putting on a doll wedding of their own.

In later years my friends would tell me that they thought I came from the perfect family, that my parents were the kind of parents they always wished they'd had. I'm sure their fantasies about us were fueled by events like the doll wedding, which must have seemed wonderfully inventive to them. The fact was my parents were not perfect, and my childhood was riddled with as much pain as any other. But I now understand how the impact of this mini-spectacle on their girlish minds could have made them regard my family differently.

Finally, the doll wedding revealed my mother's imagination, her childlike sense of fun, which sometimes got lost amid the responsibilities of working as a schoolteacher and taking care of a household that included her husband, two children and her mother.

You might say it was the power of her imagination that infused much of my childhood. Its spark was always there, and it created magic for me in other ways than just a doll's wedding at Christmas. Not just her love of dolls, but also her love of books, which I inherited, and her love of music. She was a music teacher and insisted that I start piano lessons when I was 7. I studied piano for nine years and eventually abandoned it, to her bitter disappointment. But that exposure gave me a love of music that continues to this day. My piano-playing has long since been upstaged by singing. But I do have a piano of my own, a gift from my parents. And if I had a daughter, I think I would give her a doll wedding and play the wedding march for her, too.

It is ironic the doll wedding took place in front of a grim backdrop of racial oppression that suffused my hometown of Birmingham, Ala., like a noxious vapor. As black people, we were amazingly limited by law and custom. There were so many places we couldn't go — to the downtown public library, the public parks and swimming pools, restaurants, the movie theaters, except for two black theaters and the balcony of a white one. There were so many things we couldn't do. In all of Birmingham there were three restaurants blacks could frequent: a coffeehouse owned by the local black millionaire and a couple of barbecue joints. A treat for my brother and me was to get my father to drive us to the black Dairy Queen way across town.

Yet, in the midst of this stifling atmosphere, our parents managed to create an existence for us that seemed normal. I took dance lessons, piano lessons. My family traveled north to Chicago, Detroit, New York, Washington to visit friends and relatives. There was the church, which offered ordinary people a place to shine and exert power they had no place else in the world. And there were events like the doll wedding.

Years later, after I had gone north to college and worked for a while in the Northeast, I stopped going home for Christmas. For a decade I didn't spend a single Christmas in the South. There were many reasons. Tensions within my family. The constant drain of their expectations of me. The feeling that I no longer belonged in the South, that it was a foreign country with small-minded people. Instead, like my other younger colleagues at whichever news outfit I worked at the time, I volunteered to work each Christmas Day.

But eventually the solitude of spending Christmas away from family and in the company of other holiday orphans grew wearing. I wanted to be at home for Christmas, and the city, even with all its excitement and possibilities, no longer felt like home. So I started going south again.

This year I will spend Christmas with my family, in Jacksonville, Fla., where my brother lives with his family and where my parents will come to spend Christmas Day. My niece, now 15, loves dolls, too. She owns a whole orphanage of Cabbage Patch Kids and a large contingent of Barbies. As she's grown up, I have contributed to her doll collection, taking as much pride in her growing family as my mother once did in mine. My niece takes good care of her dolls, too, just as I did. But in a few years she will leave home for college and leave her dolls behind.

One day she, too, may want to put distance between herself and her family, and probably, in time, she will want to come back. I don't know what childhood memories will draw her back, but I hope they are as vivid and magical for her as the memory of my doll's wedding is for me. Then both of us will have come full circle.

Sheryl McCarthy *joined* Newsday *in 1987 and has been a columnist for the paper since 1989. She has hosted weekly talk shows in New York, was a correspondent for ABC News and is a member of the New York Bar. A collection of her columns,* "Why Are the Heroes Always White?," *was recently published.*

Dear Santa
I have tried to be a good
boy. So I am asking you for
these toys-
TO Santa Claus TCR racing Truk
at the north pole B-17 Flying fortress
Dere Santa Claus

A Silver Box Of Memories

by Donald P. Myers

I believed in Christmas until I was eight years old.
–W.C. Fields

On the night before his seventh Christmas, my son set out cookies and milk by the fireplace and then scrawled a blue note to a fat friend: "Dear Santa, I have been very good. I want a big diamond ring and a happy family."

I keep that scribble, sheathed like a dagger, in a silver box with some of the other ghosts from seasons past. I read the note now and then, checking the words like a map that tells me where I have been and where I am going.

Because Christmas is a two-faced thing, I have been going in different directions lately. This is the season to be jolly, and it's also the sea–

son to be sad. It's the season that reminds most of us of our younger selves, when even the worst in us was once wonderful. If we had happy childhoods, we miss what we had. If we didn't, we mourn what we missed.

Some of what we had at our house hangs around in my little box of memories.

There's a faded photograph of my son and his little sister, popeyed in their pajamas on Christmas Eve. They had been alerted by a news bulletin on the radio: An unidentified flying object had been picked up on radar racing high in the northern sky, heading our way. In that photograph, the children are frozen at the front window, searching the night sky for some sign of a miniature sleigh.

There's the miniature library of Little Golden Books in the box, 39 cents each, their pages stained and sticky: "The Night Before Christmas," "Baby's Santa Mouse," "Rudolph the Red-Nosed Reindeer," "Frosty the Snowman." "A Christmas Carol," by Charles Dickens, is in there, too.

There's a crisp exchange that I wrote down on a distant winter morning. Dad: "Merry Christmas!" Daughter: "Your fly's unzipped."

There's my son's second top front tooth, wrapped in a tissue inside an envelope with a message from his mother: "10:15 p.m., adamantly stating that there is no Tooth Fairy or Santa Claus, realism sets in at age 7."

There's another biting note, left under my daughter's pillow: "Dad, if you give money for the Tooth Fairy, fold it."

There's applause from my son's third-grade teacher: "You have an extremely bright boy. He is going someplace." But where? Clipped to that note from school is something my son said that wrinkled his mother a few years later: "Have gone to Smedley's Bar and then to Sheila's Porno Palace. Back at 10."

There's a postcard scrawled under a 9-cent stamp by my daughter during her season in the sun at the beach: "Hi, Daddy. I am a surfer now. I am not me anymore."

Childhood, like a tan, fades fast, and then before you know it, wrinkles are roaming around in yesterday's peaches and cream. Dr. Seuss gives us the bad news: "Adults are obsolete children."

By the time my son turned 8, his fat friend had disappeared off the radar screen. But the year before, on the night he left food by the fireplace, if there were Christmas dreams at our house, surely they came sugarplummed. For one night, maybe there was no sadness, no fighting, no fibs. And if there was no diamond ring the next morning, at least for one last Christmas maybe there was some peace, fancy and faith in our family.

The poets tell us that we are smarter in our winter than we are in our spring, but I wonder about that. I don't think we adults know any more than our children. Maybe we've just been around longer, and experience is the name we give to our mistakes.

After her long-ago season in the sun, the little surfer told me at the airport, "I wish you and Mommy could live together. I like you both. Can't you just stop fighting?"

A good many things go around in the dark besides Santa Claus.

On the night of the blue note at our house, I ate the cookies and drank the milk around midnight, but I failed to take my son's wish as a warning. I think I gave my wife a blender on that last Christmas before the divorce.

Maybe some of us decide to have children, because, like pets, they are cute and cuddly. But if a pack of cigarettes requires a warning, shouldn't baby pictures, too?

Before I knew it, the surfer was 16, and I took her down in the morning to get her driver's license. That night she took the car out and wrecked it. And before I knew it, the cute and cuddly boy was scraping fuzz from his face with a red razor shaped like a naked lady.

A Silver Box Of Memories

Down the road from childhood at our house, it's been a long, hard gallop just to stay ahead of the posse. My son and daughter and I, among us, have wrecked seven cars. We've broken three arms, two hands, one collarbone and maybe a few hearts. We've been in the spotlight. We've been on the honor roll. We've been to the hospital. We've been in court.

Despite all the self-righteous talk these days about family values, I think most of us at Christmas come wrapped in our family flaws.

My father steered the pointed green nose of his Studebaker Champion into the 13th year of my life, and when he kissed me on the mouth, it was my first taste of whisky. His happy days tumbled from half-pints back then, and he would belt three fingers of Four Roses at a time. He would suck half a lemon to cut the burn, and he would shudder as if he had been shot.

He would light a Chesterfield with a Zippo, and his lips would leave a half-inch filter of spit on the weed. "Fiddle faddle," he would toot, and then he would smile and belch the smoke and the smells of spirit like some dandy dragon.

It was the first time I had met my father when I wasn't in diapers. I had lived for a few years in a California children's home, and I remembered my father only from unkept Christmas promises, always written in turquoise ink, always the same every year: "Send me your sizes and I will send you some clothes."

Surgeons pruned my father's pep before cancer killed him a month before Christmas 26 years ago. He was 56. He had been a traveling knickknack salesman, peddling ceramic cats and dogs across the Southwest, through Truth or Consequences and Sweetwater and Durango. With a mug of soap and a strop and a straight razor, he taught me how to shave. He showed me the route to a demon pot of stew. And he introduced me to the heights of a barstool and a ginger ale with a swizzle stick and a twist.

My father and I talked about home runs and halfbacks, but we never spoke of feeling scared or sad or sorry or examined much of anything besides three-fingered solutions. I don't remember us ever saying "I love you" out loud. Maybe we thought we would live forever.

My father gave me his last smile when needles brought him happy days. I bathed him with a washrag and a pan of cool water in his hospital bed in the summer scorch of Texas, and then I lathered his cheeks and his chin and shaved off his whiskers.

"I guess I look good enough to die," he said, slowly and softly, into a mirror he held with the hand that had written me turquoise promises, and I smoothed Old Spice aftershave across my father's smile. He had joshed me about avoiding marriage and delaying his grandchildren, but when I accomplished both, when my son and my daughter were born, my father was gone.

Becoming a parent isn't hard, but being one is. We commit old sins in new ways.

"Bouncing me around between you and Mom — I wasn't too crazy about that," my son tells me on the telephone. "If I was living with Mom, I'd go see you. If I was living with you, I'd visit her. It always had to end. That's what Christmas means to me, saying good-bye."

If the son swears, do we strike the father? If the news is bad, do we beat the messenger? If the shoe fits, do we wear it?

When I was a boy wearing braces, the kids in choir called me Tinsel Teeth. I was an 11-year-old soprano, and we were all singing the sappy new holiday hit, "All I Want for Christmas Is My Two Front Teeth."

The choirboy would croak that year. Innocence died with Babe Ruth. It was the year the Cold War cranked up. And it was the year I stopped believing in Christmas.

Following yonder star, Melchior, Caspar and I had cameled into the Christmas pageant at school. We Three Kings of

Orient Were, and I was Balthasar in blue britches, crowned by a crew cut. As the make-believe Magi climbed the stairs to the stage, I turned away from the manger toward my mother's smile.

Balthasar tripped on the top stair and fell flat on his adoration.

My turban, a towel, unraveled. My tin of myrrh, some water, clattered all the way across the stage into the wings. My choir robe ripped. One of my shoes came off. The auditorium laughed. My teeth twinkled in the spotlight.

We Three Kings were We Three Stooges.

Later, out in the hall while I was kicking my locker, my mother tried to console her weeping wise kid. "I know it looks like the end of the world now," she told me, "but someday you will be able to laugh at this."

My mother was right, bless her. Given my performance as a father, when I think of myself as a wise man in a turban, it's really pretty funny. I stopped believing in Christmas in that last season of the soprano, but not for long. The next spring, dimpled little Pauline Murray gave me something new to sing about. She kissed me. The hormones were cranking up with the Cold War, and by the next Christmas I had fallen all the way into the baritone section.

The choirboy had become a rascal.

We rascals get a little rank at this time of year. W.C. Fields stopped believing in Christmas the year he saved up to buy his mother a present, then hid the cash in the coal bin. "My father found

it," he said later. "He did exactly what I would have done in his place. He stole the money."

Given the mutilations of our childhoods, it's a wonder any of us can be jolly in this stained and sticky season. At my house, if we don't search the night sky for a miniature sleigh anymore, at least we still have a little faith and fancy. The posse, after all, hasn't been on our tail for a good long time now.

My son believed in Santa Claus until the year he turned 8, but his sister kept the faith a while longer. I told them when they went away to college that I thought they should be separated from their parents by at least two mountain ranges. I think that's about the only advice they ever took from me.

My son, the Colorado retro-hippie and mountain biker, is 24 now. My daughter, 22, the Oregon college student and cocktail waitress, plans to teach history. They are home for the holidays, and we still do a lot of childish things. My daughter offers cookies and milk by the fireplace. She knows I like chocolate chips.

Getting up and down the chimney isn't as easy as it used to be.

We aren't popeyed in our pajamas anymore, but I'm sure we'll still prowl around in my silver box of memories on Christmas — and stop by Smedley's Bar and Sheila's Porno Palace. Then the three of us will try to cook a yuletide goose.

"I love you," my son now tells me out loud.

Donald P. Myers joined Newsday as a feature writer in 1988. He is a native of Texas, and spent 16 years at UPI, including a stint as managing editor for news. He also has worked for papers in Denver, Miami and Portland, Ore.

The Curse Of The Santa Suit

by Cal Fussman

"Y ou have to do it," she said, sliding the baggy red pants up my legs.

"Yeah, but . . ."

"You're the guest. You're the one the grandchildren are least likely to recognize." She brought the big buckle around my waist and hitched it closed. "Is that comfortable?"

"But isn't there . . ."

"Make sure the mustache doesn't fluff up into your nose," she said, taping the white beard into place. "You don't want to sneeze on the kids."

She topped my head with a red furry cap and turned me toward the mirror. "There — you see, you look great."

The Curse Of The Santa Suit

I stared into the mirror. Yup, I was Santa all right. Why, I wondered, did I feel so uneasy? Perhaps every Jew in a Santa Claus suit for the first time feels this way, I thought, dismissing the feeling.

"You'll be great, don't worry," Janine said.

There was no way out. Besides, how could I turn the family down after all they were giving me?

See, I'd never scrambled down a staircase toward a tinseled tree, or examined a plate of cookie crumbs left near the fireplace, or watched euphoric nephews and nieces dive into stacks of presents. Suddenly, at age 32, the wonderful cliché of a Merry Christmas was being handed to me like a gift with bows. My friend Gary had opened the door to his family's home in a cheerful suburb of Wilmington, Del. And his parents, four brothers, four sisters and all those grandchildren embraced me. Next thing I knew, one of his sisters was shepherding me out the back door in a Santa Claus suit and handing me a fistful of bells.

"Hey, listen!" the parents gasped as I jingled the bells out-side. "It's Santa Claus!"

As I bounded through the front door, all the grandchildren's eyes popped wide with belief. I "Ho! Ho! Hoed!" They squealed. I asked them what they wanted. They each hopped into my lap and requested $400 worth of toys. I inhaled deeply and told them Santa would try his best. After a few minutes I was exiting the front door, and the parents were staring out the living room window with hands cupped over their eyes — waving goodbyes to the reindeer floating off into the sky. It was all quite ordinary, no different from the millions of other appearances Santa annually made around America. Yes, I probably would have forgotten the experience altogether if my tongue hadn't turned green a few months later, or perhaps if my fiancée hadn't then called off our engagement two weeks before the wedding.

I was still in a daze when the next Christmas at the Smiths rolled around.

"Hey, you were great last year," one of Gary's brothers said trying to cheer me up. "Can you be Santa again?"

I felt myself recoil without quite knowing why. Oh, I'm a little under the weather, I said, my voice turning nasal. You definitely don't want me close to all those kids right now.

And so Gary's sister, Janine, dropped her voice a few octaves and "Ho! Ho! Hoed!" through the front door. Janine's life was a happy Hallmark card. Married to a handsome dentist, she lived in a beautiful home and had a challenging job.

Within weeks after Janine stepped into the Santa suit, the dentist demanded a divorce, disappearing with one of his hygienists.

Now, I'm a logical guy. And, yes, it seemed absurd at first. But even back then I couldn't help but wonder: Was it the suit? I felt like I had to do something. But who was I, an outsider, to halt a family tradition? Still, what if the suit was cursed? How could I put anyone else at risk? I arrived early for the next holiday celebration at the home of the couple who stored the suit in their attic, sister Sue and brother-in-law Tommy, and asked them to replace it.

"Don't be silly," Tommy harrumphed. Tommy is an insurance agent, a man whose business operates on statistics and probability charts. "I'm not going to go out and buy a new Santa Claus suit just because of your nonsensical phobias."

"Look, it's two years in a row," I said. "First me, then Janine. Please, trust me on this."

"Nothing's going to happen. I can prove it. A few days ago, we loaned the suit out to our next-door neighbor, Hugh."

"YOU DID WHAT?"

"Calm down. He gave a performance for the kids at the local recreation center. The kids had a great time. Nothing bad happened. He returned the suit just yesterday — everything's fine. And

The Curse Of The Santa Suit

Janine's new boyfriend, Rick, is going to play Santa at our party."

I knew trouble was headed for the family's next Santa as soon as I saw him. Janine's new boyfriend, Rick, owner of a hair salon, was a pleasant, gentle guy, the sensitive sort. Easy meat for the Santa suit.

The inevitable, of course, soon occurred. Rick was dumped by Janine and, not long after, his hair salon went bankrupt. Then came news of the neighbor, Hugh, who'd borrowed the suit. You guessed it. Hugh's gallbladder.

When I showed up for the next Christmas with a clove of garlic around my neck, the family hooted and jeered. By this time I was seen as the family's eccentric, just another cog in the Smith family tradition. You could count on Brent, the youngest son, to slink over to you each year and ask for a $3,000 loan to help finance a BMW. You could count on Alison, the daughter up from Texas, to burble on and on about how her son Chad had just learned to color between the lines or master some brainless task in phonics. And you could count on Cal to howl about the evil lurking in that Santa Claus suit. Somehow it felt good to have a dependable role, to know I was an important fixture in the yearly ritual.

"Don't start on me again," growled Tommy the life insurance agent. "It's all a figment of your imagination."

"It was no figment of my imagination when my fiancée called the wedding off."

"She acted perfectly reasonably," Tommy said. "What sane woman would marry you?"

"And what about my tongue?"

He scowled. "You go into the Amazon jungle on vacation and you get bit by some exotic insect that gives you a rash and turns your tongue green. So what?"

"Oh yeah, and Janine's marriage to Bob?"

"What's the divorce rate in this country? Fifty percent?

Besides — good riddance. I knew that guy was no good from the start. Look at what he did to Gary's teeth."

"Individually, you can mock the examples. But you can't deny the sheer weight of evidence. What about Rick's business? What about Hugh?"

"Hey, we're in a recession. If Donald Trump is going belly up, what do you expect from Rick? And do you know how many people in this country have gallbladder operations each year? Perhaps you should call The New England Journal of Medicine. I'm sure they'd be quite interested to research a theory linking gallbladder surgery to Santa Claus suits."

I sat back, flushed with exasperation, and sipped my beer. Maybe Tommy was right. Maybe break-ups and bankruptcies and burst bladders were just everyday life. Maybe Christmas was merely a few days of being thankful for surviving all the problems that happen to us year-round.

"Would you just relax and enjoy Christmas?" Tommy said.

"I don't know." It was Sue, Tommy's wife, coming to my rescue. "To be honest, I'm getting a little leery about letting anyone in the family wear that suit."

"You too?" Tommy rolled his eyes. "Okay, okay, okay . . . I have an idea," he said. We'll ask Donnie to be Santa this year.

"Donnie!"

At the risk of offending every family, every family has its Donnie. He's the one with the booming voice, the one who beat you once at whiffle ball when you were 7 years old and still booms about it 30 years later. He was family, yes, but not direct family — the brother of a brother-in-law — and because he had always been with his own family in the past when Santa appeared at the Smith residence, Donnie knew nothing of the curse.

No one could argue. Not even me. He was the perfect candidate.

The Curse Of The Santa Suit

Who can possibly explain what happened to Donnie two days after he wore the suit? Who can explain it when a man leaves his parents' house carrying all his and his wife's Christmas gifts, packs them in the car and goes to wish Merry Christmas to a friend who happens to be a state policeman — only to emerge from the policeman's house an hour later and discover that not one of his wife's presents has been touched, but that every one of his own gifts except a pair of athletic socks with holes in them has been stolen?

Who can explain it when a man, still smarting from such a loss, goes to his beach house to see in the New Year with a crackling blaze in the fireplace, sweeps all the dead embers into a brown paper bag, places it in the utility room with the rest of the trash, just as he has done dozens of other times, and sits down to enjoy a football game — only to look over and discover a strange glow beneath his utility room door?

What logical rationale is there for the sight of a 38-year-old man racing to the front door clutching a fiery brown paper bag, spewing flames that burn holes in his carpet, melt his vinyl kitchen floor and vacuum cleaner hose while his wife streaks from the shower to try to extinguish the blaze without a stitch of clothing on and ax-wielding firefighters storm the neighbor's condominium door?

I got a phone call just a few days ago. "You coming to celebrate Christmas?" Tommy the life insurance agent asked.

"Well . . .," I hesitated.

"Don't worry," Tommy said. "Everyone finally believes you. You can relax this year."

"What do you mean?"

"We got rid of the suit."

I could feel the emptiness spreading through the pit of my stomach before I'd even hung up the phone. Sure, I'd go again. But Christmas at the Smiths would never be the same.

Cal Fussman, after a decade traveling through Europe reporting for The Washington Post and Life magazine, became a feature writer at Newsday. He is now a senior writer at ESPN Magazines and a contributor to many publications.

Gift For
Giving

by Paul Vitello

The first I remember of him, I am about 4 and he is about 64. He is walking in, carrying some shopping bags full of gifts. It is an image as clear as day, though maybe too clear for it to be literally true. Maybe it is a composite stitched together from many entrances made by my grandfather, who was the best entrance-maker of anybody in my childhood, when first impressions were everything.

He is wearing a long wool coat, a fedora, a silk scarf and a necktie; and my cousins and I are jumping into his arms, one at a time, to be enveloped in his embrace and in the delicious cold air that clings to his coat and face. Our hands are in his pockets. Our hands are on his hat, which we love to snatch and mash and hide. We are like monkeys, my cousins and I, and he is our leader. Grownups, shooing us

Gift For Giving

away, help him off with his coat.

My grandfather was an interesting man in a lot of ways, most of which I would only learn about later, when I was considered old enough to grasp a little bit about politics and religion. He was a freethinker, a talker, a man with hundreds of friends, an atheist, a believer in mankind with a capital M.

But in the memory of this grandson, he was the grownup, more than any other, who understood Christmas.

It was a pretty simple Christmas vision, as I understood it then and still do. To my grandfather, Christmas was about Christmas presents.

As best I could tell, he loved thinking about them, buying them, handing them out, carrying them in big shopping bags to the gatherings on Christmas Eve in the far-flung apartments of his children and grandchildren all over Manhattan and Brooklyn.

But most of all, he loved the physical excitement of opening them.

That was Frank Mandese in his glory: sitting in the middle of the floor, wrapping paper everywhere, helping a grandchild open the gift he knew that that child wanted more than anything else in the world.

I don't think he ever put a tag on a gift. We all knew which were his. They were the ones that made us feel flushed with excitement, gulping for air in the highest altitudes of Christmas pleasure.

By the time I showed up in his life he was in his 60s. But it was clear to me and my cousins, in our instinctive way, that although grandpa was bigger than us and older than us and smarter and wiser than us, he was still and all, most of all, one of us.

He loved toys. I don't believe he ever bought a child a scarf or a pair of gloves, or any other kind of Useful Thing, in his life. If there is such a thing as perfect pitch in Christmas, he had it.

He was a love matchmaker of presents and us.

It's funny to be saying this, because with a few exceptions — a Lionel train set that is still good and a night-light in the form of a cruise ship that I wish I still had — I can't really remember what most of those presents were. They were numerous. They were usually big. He loved big. And they were always right. But what I remember most is the feeling of them: the sense, when they were unwrapped, that they were things which had journeyed far and long but were finally here, where they belonged, in the grubby little hands that were meant to bring them to life.

I don't remember a word he ever spoke, which is ironic, considering what I would later learn about his prodigious appetite for conversation and discussion on matters of the world. I just remember that feeling.

He worked as a barber most of his life. In the last few years, to my delight, he worked in a barbershop in a subway station in Manhattan. This was the most exciting possible venue for any line of work, in my opinion — underground, with trains. But combined with a workplace that featured mirrors and scissors and swivel chairs that went up and down, and tall, mytserious glasses of blue water (who knew it was just disinfectant?) this was a place close to heaven.

I'm pretty sure I visited him there, although it may have been in a dream. Anyway, whenever I see a barber who still wears a white smock fastened with snaps at the shoulder, I think of him.

That is the tricky thing about early childhood memories. They get confused with things that happen later, and with things that people tell you. On top of which is always the danger of a thick, dusty layer of wishful thinking.

It is probably this trickiness that makes people's earliest holiday memories the best. They are not necessarily untrue, but filtered and distilled: two or three years compressed into one, the best of the real and the imagined standing together in the same, cozy room under the most perfect tree.

Maybe I remember Santa Claus and his reindeer painted on the mirrors of my grandfather's barbershop with paste and colored glitter. Maybe that was something I saw somewhere else.

But, certain things I can say with confidence.

Fact: Grandpa was a freethinker–barber.

Fact: He was a Christmas genius.

Fact: I was crazy about him.

I'm sure he was a good barber, though the most famous story in the family about his barbering was about him laying down the scissors and staging a strike at his brother's barbershop on the Upper West Side.

He was, as I said, a man of ideas, and at some point early on, not long after his older brothers, who had the barbershop, had sponsored his passage over from Italy, my grandfather apparently got the idea to form a union. He was in fact a charter member of a now-defunct barber's union that had its heyday in the 1920s.

As a result of this heyday, and for other reasons, our side of the family and the families of the brothers were never very close. There was probably more to it. There always is.

But I knew nothing of this when my grandfather was alive, and only learned what I did by collecting pieces of narrative scraps and string dropped here and there by the adults. That is how I would hear about his soapbox orations at Union Square in the 1920s, about his activism on behalf of the anarchists, Sacco and Vanzetti, the threats by his adopted government to see him deported if he didn't quiet down, which he did, more or less, being a man with nine children, six of whom survived childhood.

I would know almost nothing about his rich store of friends, whose numerousness and very existence I only glimpsed on the occasion of his funeral, when I was 7.

What I did know, besides my sense that he was one of us, was that grandpa Frank Mandese, my mother's father, was unique. There was nothing mysterious about how I came to this conclusion. All you had to do was walk into his apartment. No one I knew lived quite like that.

It was a railroad flat in Greenpoint, Brooklyn. I'm told it had the usual number of rooms — a living room, a couple of bedrooms, a kitchen and a bathroom.

But every square inch of wall in that place was covered with books. There were bookshelves everywhere, including the kitchen and bathroom. Bookshelves to the ceiling. He had a ladder to reach the ones on top. He owned about 4,000 books, in English and Italian, most of which the family had to give to libraries or sell to dealers when he died, though we kept some, including his well-worn volumes of Dante, the poet, Mazzini, the statesman, and Emma Goldman, the anarchist and early feminist.

I wouldn't have put it this way at the time, but at the age of 4 or 5, the sight of those books was a revelation to me. Not just that there were so many books in the world, but that someone would have the appetite to want to read so many books.

My grandfather had appetites. I wouldn't have been able to put this to words then, either, but I knew instinctively that his appetites never waned in his later years, where I came into picture, and that this was what made him and me kindred souls.

In him I recognized someone who could lose himself in the pursuit of his interests just as completely as I could lose myself in the pursuit of mine. Lucky for me, his interests included me. He poured himself into the pursuit of his grandchildren's happiness with the same passion he had for his books, and for his ideas, and for his friends, and for his politics.

That kind of appetite is a natural state in a child, a rare one in a man, and it made him a wonderful grandfather.

He left us at about this time of year. My memory on this

Gift For Giving

is pretty clear.

He had been having health problems. The kids were told that maybe grandpa would take it easy on the Christmas front this year.

It was the year that one of my cousins taught me my first lesson in empathy. Our grandfather, though he was sick, asked in the usual way what we wanted for Christmas; and while all the others kept their counsel, in accordance with the grownups' orders, I piped right in with my list.

The look of reproach she hurled at me then — she being the wiser 7½ to my 7 — was not so much withering as informative: It told me in one split second, in that glance, that there were limits to Grandpa and that it was time to grow up, which I have been trying to do ever since.

He died that December on a sidewalk in New York. The wool coat, the scarf, the tie and the fedora all were there, I'm sure. He was window-shopping for us, we were told. I'm pretty sure it's true. I know I've missed him.

Paul Vitello has been a Newsday columnist since 1986. Born in Chicago and raised on Manhattan's Lower East Side, he has worked as a reporter in Chicago, Kansas City and Albany, N.Y., and as a free-lance writer in Italy.

Bittersweet Memories Of Christmas Past

by Irene Virag

We just put up our Christmas tree, which I suspect is one of the few around with dreidels among the decorations. As I plugged in the lights and stood back to admire the result, I was reminded that Christmas is a journey of the spirit.

My noels are signposts in my life. Places in my heart. Seasons of loneliness and love, moments of missing the past, times when I knew I'd found the future. The journey of my Christmases has taken me across oceans and through sea changes, from childhood to marriage, from stuffed cabbage to cassava pie.

Bittersweet Memories Of Christmas Past

The stuffed cabbage was a beginning. It was the best stuffed cabbage I have ever eaten. In the house of my childhood in Bridgeport, Conn., my mother's stuffed cabbage and Hungarian soup took the place of the Christmas goose I learned about from reading Charles Dickens, and the turkey and roast beef I imagined were served on fine china in homes where people dressed for dinner and never yelled at each other. There was a lot of yelling in my house, especially in the days when my stepfather was drinking.

Christmas Eve was a big boozing night for my stepfather, who would come home roaring obscenities and bearing ridiculous gifts, like a fuzzy blue dog that blinked its eyes and barked and wagged its tail when you wound it up — not exactly appropriate for two adolescent daughters. Or the electric candles that still stand like sentries every December at the top of the front-porch stairs of the pink-shingled three-family house in a fading neighborhood. I was about 10 years old the Christmas he came home stinking drunk with the gaudy plastic tapers that some guy in the factory where he tended boilers sold him. I hated them, and at the time I hated him, too.

My mother and sister and I would escape on Christmas Eve to Calvin United Church of Christ, where the minister had the thick accent of his native Transylvania and wore a long black robe and got in your face when he talked. He reminded me of Bela Lugosi, and privately I thought of him as Dracula. My favorite moment came after the sermon, when soft candlelight and the sounds of silence filled the church.

For my entire life — and most of hers — my Aunt Pearl has been the organist in the church of immigrants that her father helped found, and every Christmas Eve before the lights dimmed, she'd look my way and I'd blow her a kiss. And then she'd start to play "Silent Night." Bert Kovacs, an insurance agent who had come to America as a young man, would stand by the altar and sing in Hungarian. "Csendes éj," he'd sing. "Szentséges éj. Mindenek nyugta mély . . ."

After the first verse, the congregation joined in — some of us in English, others in Hungarian. My mother, who was born in this country but didn't learn to speak English until she went to kindergarten, always sang in Hungarian. In those days I was perpetually angry at my mother for not divorcing my stepfather, but on Christmas Eve I'd hold her hand as she sang, and I'd feel warm and protected like nothing could hurt me and the world was safe — at least until the music stopped. Until the service was over and we'd walk out into the cold night and go home to the sound and fury of a man howling at demons he never understood and was never able to banish — not even after he went on the wagon. Drunk or sober, he would finish Christmas Eve sitting alone in a darkened room with tears flooding his cheeks as he watched the Pope celebrating midnight mass in the Vatican.

It made it harder that he was the only father I ever knew. Certainly he was more real than the pale man I met for the first and only time the day after Christmas when I was a junior in high school. "This your father," a grandmother I barely knew said in broken English, and I stared at a face that strangely resembled my own. The man in a wrinkled white shirt never moved from the couch in the starkly furnished living room of his parents' house. He looked past my sister and me and said hello to my mother — the woman he had abandoned years before when I was a baby. Now he had nothing for his daughters — not a word, not a smile, not even a "Merry Christmas." My sister and I walked away and sat in another room with my cousins. Fifteen minutes later we went home. We did not know where the man who looked like me had been all those years or where he would go when he left. I was 16 years old, and I used the F-word I had heard so many times in the house in Bridgeport but had never used before. "—— him," I said. "Who the —— does he think he is?" I'll never know. He never showed up again.

As grown-ups self-destructed around me, I looked for solace in the rites of the holiday. I helped stuff the meat-and-rice

68

mixture into the cooked cabbage leaves, and I peeled carrots and potatoes for the soup. I loved hanging the shiny ornaments on our Christmas tree. My sister, who was two years older, always placed the top on the tree — we didn't have an angel like most people or a twinkling star. We had a ball studded with spikes that lit up and reminded me of the golden steeple on our church but actually looked more like the morning stars that knights wielded in combat. I was astonished the year I came home from college and my mother announced she wasn't going to trim a tree. "I'm too old," she said. She was barely 50. She decorated the house with the cardboard nativity scene that was so worn it was held together with Scotch tape, and I hung all our Christmas cards around the archway that separated the living room from the dining room. My stepfather still put lights around the front porch and plugged in the two dreaded candlesticks. But I missed the tree. I was trying to go home again but my spirit was on the move.

Since then, my Yuletides have carried me to distant places in the world and the heart. I still remember the way stations. I was a college junior taking a year abroad at the University of London on a scholarship. I was backpacking in Europe with two girlfriends that winter break. We were in Germany — in a little gasthaus on the edge of the Black Forest run by an old woman with a bunch of parrots she fed homemade cookies.

On Christmas Eve, we walked in the village square and I could smell the forest, and the stars looked like diamonds sparkling in a black velvet jewel case. Snow hugged the earth and danced in the cold air. The villagers were caroling around a stately evergreen that glowed in the square. They sang a melody I had learned in the fourth grade, "O Tannenbaum, O Tannenbaum," and I joined in. We passed a toy-maker's shop with wooden trains and nutcrackers in the window, and I thought about the children in that village on the edge of the Black Forest on the night before Christmas. Were they happy, I wondered.

Were they loved? I felt so far away from my own childhood, but mostly I was awed by this great big world I was just starting to explore, a world I was sure with the arrogance of youth that I'd conquer. We went back to our gasthaus and ate bread and cheese and cold cuts we'd bought earlier that day and drank wine and sang "Silent Night" — in English.

Other Christmases marked my wandering. There were the two in Austin, Texas, where I was starting my newspaper career and wrote about Willie Nelson's second wife and he sent me four dozen roses. I volunteered to work on Christmas because I couldn't afford to go home. My parents visited me just before Thanksgiving that first year, and my mother gave me a ceramic tree she'd made in a craft workshop. Through my years of living in small apartments, it would be my only Christmas tree.

I spent those Christmases writing stories about the sad and the lonely and the poor and the sick. I wrote about Christmas at a battered-women's shelter and about an Alcoholics Anonymous meeting on Christmas Eve. I'd come home to my furnished apartment after writing about Santa's visit to a hospice for children with cancer and make a cup of tea and plug in the ceramic tree and sit in the dark and think about snow. I sent home ornaments shaped like the Lone Star State that wished everyone "Merry Christmas from Deep in the Heart of Texas." I bought one for myself and wrapped it in tissue paper and wondered if I'd ever have a real tree of my own. In those days, I put Christmas trees in the same category as couches. If you owned a couch, you couldn't throw everything in the back of the car and leave town. Couches meant settling down. I was only 24 and all I had was a futon. Couches meant being grown up. Maybe they meant being happy.

I'm married now and I have a couch of my own. I have three stepchildren — one of my stepdaughters is a year older than me, and my 30-year-old stepson has hair that is longer than mine. My husband is Jewish. He has had his own Christmas journeys, and they are very different from mine. The first year we were married, I took him to the Calvin United Church of Christ on Christmas Eve. Bert Kovacs had a heart condition and he did not feel strong enough for "Csendes Éj," but a young woman sang "Silver Bells." They didn't dim the lights and Aunt Pearl was spending the winter in Arizona. It was okay, but my husband was uncomfortable in a Christian house of worship on Christmas for reasons that go back to a world neither one of us made.

And maybe, just maybe, I've grown up. I have two couches and a real Christmas tree. A big, full tree that scents the living room with joy and love and all those corny things a little girl who escaped sound and fury by hiding in her closet and reading once thought were the exclusive domain of people who dressed for dinner and never yelled at each other. People I know now don't really exist. There are colored lights and a big red bow at the top and ornaments from my childhood — two white snowballs that open up to hold dollar bills, and the silver bells that decorated my mother's tree in another place and time. There are ornaments that mark my marriage from places my husband and I have traveled together — a red and white wooden lobster pot from Maine and an American Indian dream-catcher from Santa Fe and a feathery Mardi Gras mask from New Orleans.

Three menorahs are on display in the living room, where we also keep our collection of nutcrackers. My husband has explained to me that Christmas and Chanukah are not parallel holidays. Chanukah is a festival that celebrates the defeat of a tyrant and the rededication of a temple. Still, it is a feast of lights and a time for gift-giving. We wear yarmulkes and say the Chanukah blessings and light the candles. And I mean no disrespect, but I think of it as part of my Christmas journey. I wrap presents for my husband and my grown-up kids, and fill Chanukah bags as well as Christmas stockings.

I place the gifts of two cultures side by side under the tree.

And we have evolved another tradition of our own, my husband and I. On Christmas itself, we journey to what is perhaps neutral ground. We go to Bermuda, to a gracious hotel that looks out on an aquamarine sea. We buy Bermuda onions made of papier-mâché and tiny glass bottles filled with pink sand to hang on our tree and presents of Scottish woolens and English china. A brass band plays carols on the streets of Hamilton and locals on lunch hours walk by in yellow Bermuda shorts and Santa hats. And on Christmas Eve, we eat turkey and ham and cassava pie — a sweet, nutmeg-flavored dish made from the root of the cassava plant and filled with savory meats. And it feels like Christmas.

Scars heal with time and perspective. I've come to realize that I can't change my past, and I try not to look back in anger. Across the years of my journey, I made my peace with my stepfather. He died last year just before Thanksgiving and I spoke at his funeral and said that he had a talent for fury. I said that he fought his own devils throughout his life and that he finally defeated the bottle. I said that I loved him. And I quoted the rage he expressed in his hospital bed the night before he died as he cursed the cancer that wasted his lungs. I'm sure it was the first time anyone had used the word "bastard" from the pulpit of Calvin United Church of Christ.

And so now I am in another place at Christmas. In fact and in mind. Bert Kovacs has moved to Arizona and my Aunt Pearl is fighting pancreatic cancer and the new minister in the church of my childhood looks nothing like Dracula. Dreidels glisten among the colored lights and silver bells on a real tree and I have gone from stuffed cabbage to cassava pie.

Christmas is a journey of the spirit and I am still traveling.

Irene Virag is Newsday's garden and nature columnist. She is also the author of a book about breast cancer, based on a series she wrote for the paper. She was a member of the Newsday reporting team that won the Pulitzer Prize for local reporting in 1984.